Sugar Spinelli's Little Instruction Book

Have to admit, this one has style. The way he has that tux jacket slung over his shoulder...very devil-may-care. And carrying a stuffed toy polar bear dressed in a tux to match his is a really nice touch!

Says he runs a toy company. That explains the polar bear. And he likes kids. He also likes that redhead in the front row, by the looks of things. Now she seems real determined, but she's gotta have some stiff competition. Let the games begin!

Dear Reader,

We just knew you wouldn't want to miss the news event that has all of Wyoming abuzz! There's a herd of eligible bachelors on their way to Lightning Creek—and they're all for sale!

Cowboy, park ranger, rancher, P.I.—they all grew up at Lost Springs Ranch, and every one of these mavericks has his price, so long as the money's going to help keep Lost Springs afloat.

The auction is about to begin! Young and old, every woman in the state wants in on the action, so pony up some cash and join the fun. The man of your dreams might just be up for grabs!

Marsha Zinberg
Editorial Coordinator, HEART OF THE WEST

His Bodyguard
Muriel
Jensen

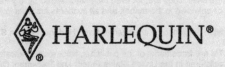

HARLEQUIN®

TORONTO • NEW YORK • LONDON
AMSTERDAM • PARIS • SYDNEY • HAMBURG
STOCKHOLM • ATHENS • TOKYO • MILAN • MADRID
PRAGUE • WARSAW • BUDAPEST • AUCKLAND

Muriel Jensen is acknowledged as the author of this work.

ISBN 0-373-82588-9

HIS BODYGUARD

Copyright © 1999 by Harlequin Books S.A.

Visit us at www.romance.net

Printed in U.S.A.

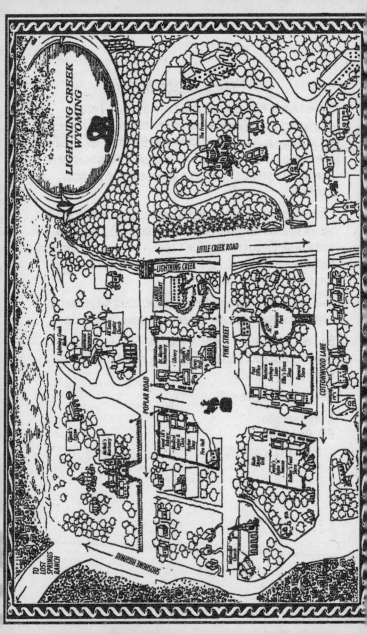

A Note from the Author

I loved Amos Pike the moment I saw his face. I create characters by finding likenesses in a magazine and posting them above my computer. After studying them for a while I see beyond the toothpaste or designer clothes they were intended to promote and get a glimpse of the person inside.

I found Amos in a dress shirt, slacks and suspenders in a men's fashion magazine. He looked thoughtful and sexy, and a little bit bored. He didn't appear to *need* a bodyguard, but life—and, therefore, fiction—is about getting what you get instead of what you want.

Meg was in a shampoo advertisement, fresh faced and eager, looking as though she needed something to do.

So I put Amos in the arena at the Lost Springs Ranch for Boys benefit auction, and Meg in the crowd with bidding money in her hands.

Here's what happened!

Muriel Jensen
P.O. Box 1168
Astoria, Oregon 97103

To Ros and Jon Lund—good companions and great fun!

CHAPTER ONE

"YOU VOLUNTEERED ME for *what?*" Amos Pike lay sprawled on his stomach on the beige-carpeted floor of his office. He was looking up in dismay from a half-constructed toy lunar module to focus on Jeannette Boradino, his administrative assistant.

She smiled. He always worried when she smiled. She ran the business offices of the Pike's Pickled Pepper Toy Company with the precision of a military operation and the no-nonsense attitude of a general. Clients loved her because she got things done, employees respected her because they knew where they stood with her, and manufacturers feared her because she accepted no excuses. Tall and statuesque and always impeccably attired in a neutral-color suit, she had the physical presence to back up her approach to business.

At 41, she'd had almost twenty years' experience in office management, four of them with Amos. She never smiled unless she had something to put to him that she knew he wouldn't like.

"I volunteered you for a bachelor auction." She dropped a folder on his desk and tapped it with the tip of her forefinger. "Airline tickets and itinerary." Then she walked briskly across his office and adjusted the blinds to let in more sunlight. "Don't forget you have lunch at the Top of the Mark at one o'clock with the Dream Stores people. I have a lunch date myself. I'll try to be back punctually, but it's with the head-master at Kyle's school, and he does tend to go on." She headed toward the door.

Amos was on his feet and in her path in one swift, easy move. "Not so fast, Jeannette." Usually relaxed and unflappable, he did his best to look severe. And when he thought about parading down a runway while women assessed his attributes, looking severe wasn't difficult.

"I've asked you not to commit me to anything without checking with me first." He frowned down at her. "You're usually very good about that."

She cleared her throat and tried to stare him down. "In this case, I thought I'd save both of us a lot of time. It's a charity event for the Lost Springs Ranch for Boys. I knew if I asked you, you'd say no, then your conscience would plague you because you've always contributed to every other fund-raiser they've approached you for. Then you'd change your mind when I'd already told them you wouldn't do it, and I'd have to call back and say you would, and they'd have to readjust their plans. This was easier."

He stared back at her. "You're fired."

She blanched. And blinked. Then her lips parted in disbelief. He saw her struggle against panic.

"I am not," she said, her voice a little high-pitched.

"All right, you're not." He shook his index finger at her. "That was just to remind you which one of us is in charge here. I thought we'd already been through this with the bodyguard thing.''

"A bodyguard is a good idea. You should have let me handle..."

"Jeannette," he interrupted firmly. "No one *handles* me. Not bodyguards, not strong women, not competitors out to beat me with trickery rather than talent. I have been looking out for myself for a long time. I'm good at it. Now, would you like to take another approach on this auction thing?''

Amos didn't know much about Jeannette's personal life, except that her husband had abandoned her before she came to work at Pike's, and she had a twelve-year-old son in a private school. He didn't know whether her tough-as-nails approach had developed before or after her husband left.

He only knew that to prevent her from steamrolling him, he had to be tougher than she was. She seemed to respect that.

She swallowed and put a hand up to smooth her short dark hair. She was herself again. "The Lost Springs Ranch called yesterday while you were in the production meeting and asked if you'd participate in a bachelor auction to raise money to save the facility.''

Save it? He had a running mental image of seesaws and nickel-pipe jungle gyms, the sage-and-sweet-grass Wyoming landscape—he could almost smell it now, as if he were there—and boys of all ages and descriptions, with one thing in common: they were as lost as the springs that had given the place its name.

"What do you mean, save it? What happened?''

She pointed to the folder on his desk. "Lindsay Duncan, the ranch's owner, faxed some details. Apparently the place has come on hard times and she's hoping the auction will help them with their financial difficulties. They've invited a number of former residents, including you, to come back and save the day."

Amos had another mental image of those boys with whom he'd played and scrapped and dug his way out of despair, and wondered what kind of adults they'd become. He was intrigued by the possibility of finding out.

He stepped over the lunar module and snagged the folder off his desk.

Jeannette picked up his empty coffee cup. "I'll refill this while you look that over. I'm...sorry if I overstepped. I thought it was important."

He sank into his high-backed leather chair and gave her an even look. "I think so, too, so there was no reason to go around me. There is never a reason to go around me."

She nodded docilely. "I understand."

He studied her suspiciously for a moment, then turned his attention to the letter from Lindsay Duncan.

Jeannette walked out of the office with a determined step.

"YOU'RE SURE YOU'RE UP to this, Meggie?" It was the fourth time Meg Loria's father had asked the question since he'd picked her up for the meeting. "I know how hard it has to be for you with—you know—having to cancel everything. But we really need you on this one."

"It's all right, Dad," Meg replied under her breath as she followed the maître d' through a sea of tables.

She was sure they didn't need her at all, that this was simply an effort to distract her from having been left at the altar.

Well, it hadn't literally been the altar, it had been the courthouse. Daniel was supposed to have met her there to get their wedding license two days ago and he'd never showed.

Certain he'd simply been delayed by a client, she'd called the law offices of Dalton, Emery and Flannigan and learned that as of that morning, they were simply Dalton and Flannigan. Emery had taken off with someone named Cloris Biederman for her summer home on Maui.

Having her fiancé run off with another woman had been hard enough, but when that woman was fifteen years *older* than Meg, it was traumatic.

Daniel's fax, waiting for her when she got home, said that he would always consider her his friend, but that he'd come to realize she didn't have a romantic bone in her body.

"You get better scores on the pistol range than I do," the fax had further criticized, "and you can throw me three out of three. I'm sorry, Meg. Cloris doesn't know which end of a gun shoots, and when I put my arms around her, she falls into them. She doesn't throw me through a plate-glass window."

What did he expect? When a woman was a trained security specialist, a man should think twice about surprising her from behind on a dark street in Chinatown. Meg had tried to explain that. But neither Daniel nor Jade Wing, whose tea-shop window Daniel had sailed through, had understood.

Meg forced her thoughts back to the moment when the maître d' stopped at a table occupied by an attractive woman Meg guessed to be in her mid-thirties. The woman had gotten to her feet at their approach and now studied Meg with a frown.

Meg's father reached around her to offer his hand to the woman. "Ms. Boradino? I'm Paul Loria, of Loria Security."

The woman smiled and took his hand. "Hello. Thank you for meeting me on such short notice."

"Of course. Ms. Boradino, this is my daughter, Margaret."

The woman shook hands with Meg, then pointed her to the chair across from her. "Please. Sit down." She reached for the arms of her own chair and was momentarily distracted when Meg's father walked around to seat her with courtly charm. She stared at him a moment, then thanked him.

"You're very young," she said to Meg as her father took his place at a right angle to them. "I'm not sure this will work. Mr. Loria, I explained that the situation is dangerous."

Meg drew a breath for patience and smiled. Rejection on all fronts was making her weirdly philosophical.

"I'm twenty-six, Ms. Boradino," she confided. "A better shot than my brothers, and I can take you down faster than my father could." At the woman's startled look and her father's quick clearing of his throat, she added quickly, "Not that he'd try to, of course. And...not you, specifically."

Despite Ms. Boradino's very formal manner, amusement flickered in her eyes. "Thank you for clarifying that. But when you're forty-one, twenty-six *is* very young. And I don't mean to diminish your skills, but the people I'm hiring protection against are ruthless and rather large. And...if my boss found out who you are..." She suddenly lost her air of control, reached to the middle of the table for a bread stick and snapped it in half. "Let's just say the bad guys won't be your only problem."

Meg smiled flatly at her father. "Thanks, Dad. I've always wanted an assignment where I'm in danger from our client as well as whoever's threatening him."

"Now, let's just think about this," Paul began placatingly. "There's no reason he has to find out you're protecting him." He smiled at Ms. Boradino. "That's the problem, isn't it? He doesn't *want* protection?"

The discussion was halted temporarily when a waiter arrived with menus and to take their order for beverages. Her father, familiar with the menu, decided they should select their lunch choices, too, and made suggestions to Ms. Boradino, who looked at him as though completely fascinated.

It was the Old World charm, Meg knew. Though third generation Italian-American, Paul Loria had been raised with European manners and style. He'd tried to raise his children in the same way, but Meg's three brothers were hopelessly contemporary, and

Meg herself didn't seem to be able to find a place where she felt comfortable.

When the waiter gathered up menus and headed off to the kitchen, Paul nodded at their client. "Start from the beginning. Tell us everything we should know about your boss so that we can all be sure we're doing the right thing here."

Ms. Boradino smiled ruefully. "It's difficult to describe Amos Pike. To say he's a self-made man is an understatement because that only implies business success and wealth. And though he's achieved both, his most admirable qualities have nothing to do with that. He's a wonderful boss because he knows what he wants and he insists upon it from you, and yet he manages to help you give it to him in the way you work best."

For someone who found it difficult to describe him, Meg thought, she was doing a thorough job. And an insightful one.

Her father apparently thought so, too. "Are you in love with him?" he asked gently.

Even Meg turned to him in surprise.

At the woman's startled look, he replied with a kind smile, "With lives at stake, it's important that we know everything. Relationships can make small but significant changes in our approach."

Meg concluded that was hogwash. Her father was interested in their client and wanted to know what or who stood in his way.

Ms. Boradino shook her head. "I'm seven years older than he is."

Paul shrugged as though that were negligible. "A

young man delights in a woman with experience. Just as an older man can find rejuvenation with a younger woman.''

Meg held back a wince at her own recent proof of his claim.

Her father seemed to realize what he'd said and cast her a quick, apologetic glance.

She shrugged her forgiveness.

"We're friends," Ms. Boradino said. Then she seemed to reconsider. "Well, not precisely. I have trouble letting people get that close." Then she glanced at Paul and at Meg, clearly startled that she'd admitted that much. She went on briskly. "He's the finest man I know, as a businessman and as a human being, and I don't want him to be hurt because of his own stubborn pride." She seemed suddenly to notice the two halves of bread stick in her hands and dropped them onto her bread plate. Then she dusted off her fingers.

"He's a toy manufacturer," she said. "You've heard of Pike's Pickled Pepper Toy Company?"

When Paul shook his head, Meg nodded. "Yes, you have, Dad. You bought that little boy next door the castle where you put the water in the moat and sea monsters go around in it. Remember? That was a Pike product."

Ms. Boradino brightened. "That's right. That was our bestseller last year." She sobered again as quickly. "Competition for the toy market has always been very intense, but since the development of Amos's Interactive Space Station, I'm afraid it could become…deadly."

"Why do you say that?" Paul asked.

"It's all been top secret, of course," she replied calmly, though she fiddled nervously with a fork. "We even missed the February toy show in favor of this later one here in San Francisco. Amos needed to refine the software that comes with the station after NASA agreed to give him some data." She put the fork down and met Paul's eyes, then Meg's. "There was a mysterious fire at our factory and a break-in at our office, and Amos was mugged by four men in his condo's parking garage. Fortunately, one of the other residents was returning with a couple of friends and the muggers took off. I think someone was out to get the designs for the station, so Amos finally hid them. Even I don't know what he's done with them, or with the prototype."

"But why the muggers?" Meg asked. "Did they think he had the plans on him?"

"Perhaps," Ms. Boradino replied. "Or maybe it was just...revenge."

"But that's getting pretty personal for a business intrigue."

Ms. Boradino spread her hands. "That was what made me suspect Jillian Chambers."

Meg nodded, waiting for her to explain.

"She's the CEO of Chayco Toys," Ms. Boradino elaborated. "Pike's only real competition in the toy market. She and Amos used to see each other—until Amos found her photographing his designs at his home one night after they'd...been together." Ms. Boradino looked skeptical. "She still insists he misunderstood her intentions. That she was designing something similar and wanted to match the plan to hers to see if they could coordinate their designs for a joint project.''

Paul made a scornful sound. "Pretty thin excuse."

"She's been trying to get him back ever since," Ms. Boradino continued, "but he doesn't deal well with having been lied to or deceived." She smiled wryly at Meg. "So you'll have to be careful."

The waiter arrived with a carafe of gewürztraminer and poured three glasses. When he left, Boradino said with a worried frown, "My real concern is that Jillian, who has always been high-strung and impulsive, has taken a dangerous turn. Her business is in trouble and I'm afraid she blames Amos for it. I wouldn't be surprised if her intentions have changed from simply trying to get him back to ruining him. And everybody in the business is waiting to see the space station demonstrated at the upcoming toy show. The software allows a child to take trips from the space station in over a dozen directions, both factual and fictitious.''

Her voice had risen in excitement, but now fell as she added, "If Jillian can prevent him from being there with it, she can ruin him. It's taken a great financial investment to get this far with it, and Amos has an electronics company waiting for the word to start production, depending on the reaction at the show."

"Okay, you're convinced the situation is desperate." Meg leaned toward the woman. "Why is it so hard for Pike to see this? If there's been a fire and a mugging and an attempt to copy his plans, and he *still* doesn't want protection, I don't see what we can do for him. When's the toy show?''

"The weekend after the bachelor auction.''

Meg was confused. "What bachelor auction?''

"That's part of the plan Ms. Boradino has come up with.'' Paul raised his glass in a toast. "And it's really rather a clever one. Shall we toast it?''

Boradino raised her glass to his.

Meg didn't. "I think I'd like to hear the plan first.''

Paul lowered his glass with a shake of his head at their client. "Meg's very methodical. Gets that from her mother. She's never one to be surprised by the unknown, and exasperating as that can be for those of us in her personal life, it's an invaluable quality in a bodyguard.''

Boradino, too, lowered her glass. "I understand completely.'' She studied Meg a moment, as though measuring her ability to carry out whatever it was she had in mind. Then, apparently deciding Meg was capable, she went on to explain.

"I tried to hire bodyguards for Amos after the mugging, and he sent them away. His entire administrative staff has been worried about him. Without his knowledge, the men have taken turns following him home at night, watching his condo, watching the plant. Someone stays all night in the office.'' She sighed, then smiled in self-deprecation. "We don't really know what we're doing, but we felt better knowing he had someone watching out for him. Then the Lost Springs Ranch for Boys called me about the bachelor auction they're having this weekend. If they don't get out of debt, they may have to sell out to a consortium.

Amos spent eight years there as a child. They've invited back the former residents who are still single. I accepted for him without asking him first because a plan began to hatch in my head.''

Paul pointed a finger at his wineglass. ''A plan worth toasting, Meg. If you bid on him and win, you can take him to the cabin on the lake until the toy show next weekend, and he won't even know he's being guarded.'' To Boradino, he added in an aside, ''My brother lived in Casper and he and I bought an old house together on Bluebell Lake in the Bighorns for fishing vacations.''

Meg considered her father's plan and experienced very real trepidation. ''Dad, what man would want to take off for a week to a cabin in the woods with a woman he's never seen before? One who's bought him at an auction!''

Paul laughed lightly. ''Almost any man I can think of.''

''Dad...''

He put a hand over hers on the table. ''Meggie, use your imagination. You can tell him you want fishing lessons, or a hiking companion, or you want to write a book about him. You can do this.''

That's what he thought. She hadn't shown him Daniel's fax. What would a woman who was purported not to have a romantic bone in her body do with a successful young executive in a mountain cabin for a week?

Okay. There were a hundred creative answers to that question. But, those aside, what else could she do without making him suspicious?

"If you can't help," Boradino said, shamelessly placing the responsibility on Meg's shoulders, "then I'm out of ideas. I don't know where to turn. You're the only chance we have of keeping him safe."

Meg put a hand to her forehead, where a throbbing pain had beaten since she'd made the call from the courthouse to Daniel's law office two days ago. Another drumming had begun in counterpoint. "What kind of scenario could I possibly make believable? I can't pass myself off as an heiress. I just don't have the…" She didn't know what it was. She just knew she didn't have it.

"He doesn't like heiresses," Boradino said, leaning toward her as though they were alone at a pajama party and indulging in a woman's favorite topic. "He likes women who are real because he's very real himself. Unfortunately, many of the women in his social circle are more interested in what he can do for them, rather than what they can do together." She studied Meg closely, then added after a moment, "I think he'd find an honest, unpretentious woman refreshing. And once you've bought and paid for him—" she smiled wickedly "—he sets his own limits on what he'll do for you. But I know him to be reckless and daring. He steps aside for no one. He'll go with you to wherever this cabin is you were talking about."

"And when he finds out it was all a setup?"

"The plan is mine. I'm the one who'll have to answer for it."

The whole idea was crazy. Meg had gained a reputation as the methodical one in her family because her life seemed to have been drafted on the principles of Murphy's Law. Everything that could go wrong did—and frequently.

She could keep Amos Pike safe. She was sure of that. But she was worried about her ability to attract him in the first place, to convince him to take off with her for a week in the wilderness.

And even if he did go with her out of a sense of duty, she knew her own limitations. Her mother died when she was ten and she'd grown up in a family of men. While she wasn't entirely unattractive, she didn't know how to make the most of her attributes, partly because she never thought about them.

She worked for her father, and she spent her spare time teaching martial arts and other classes in the Women in Transition program at the community college. She lived her life in sweats, watching for trouble. Not the best way to meet men.

"Of course," her father prodded as he swirled the contents of his glass, "if you think you'll need backup, I could get Ben or Brian to..."

"No. Thanks." That was dirty. He'd done it deliberately to force her hand. Meg's brothers were the kindest, dearest men on the face of the earth, and the bane of her professional life. They were incapable of believing she could handle an assignment without one of them looking in on her. She hated that. And her father knew it.

"And I'm supposed to outbid wealthy women," she asked him, "on what you pay me?"

Boradino straightened hopefully in her chair and Paul smiled. "Ms. Boradino's taking care of that with the help of the rest of the administrative staff and other...undesignated company funds.''

Meg could imagine how much Pike must mean to this woman if she was willing to risk his wrath by tricking him with a bodyguard and using "undesignated" company funds with which to do it.

Somehow, Meg couldn't find it in her to fail this woman. She picked up her wineglass. ''To Ms. Boradino's plan.''

"Bless you!'' Boradino said, touching her glass to Meg's, then to Paul's.

Meg's father smiled fondly at his daughter. "You're going to have a good time with this, Meggie.''

"Mmm,'' she replied. "I can hardly wait.''

CHAPTER TWO

"RED OR BLACK?" Becky Winston, director of the Women in Transition program at Wild Hills Community College, opened her wardrobe closet and pulled out two cocktail dresses. The red one was slinky and sequined, the black layered in chiffon and hanging from spaghetti straps.

Meg sat on the foot of her bed and shook her head. "They're beautiful, but it's not a formal occasion. It takes place in the afternoon and outdoors in an arena at the Lost Springs Ranch for Boys."

Becky, a half inch shorter than Meg's five-seven, and just as slender in build, had offered Meg the pick of her wardrobe when she'd complained of having nothing to wear to the auction.

She put the dresses away and pulled out beige twill trousers and a brown silk shirt, then a denim jumper that would fall just above the knee. "This looks really cute with a T-shirt. Want to try it on? You'll wow him with your legs."

Meg was about to deny that she wanted to wow Amos Pike, then remembered that she did. She had to make him want to go away with her for a week or the whole Boradino plan fell apart.

She pulled her slacks and sweater off. Becky dug

in the drawer of her dresser and handed Meg a crisp white T-shirt.

The shirt and jumper on, Meg studied her reflection in the mirrored wardrobe doors.

Becky combed her fingers through Meg's curly red hair. "What kind of impression do you want to make? Sexy? Powerful? Vampish?"

Meg remembered what Boradino had said. "I don't want to strike any poses. I just want to be me."

Becky winced. "No, you don't. Let's face it, Loria. What you are right now is Chuck Norris in a skirt. What we want him to see is the woman inside the security specialist, the part of you that would have blossomed if you'd had a mom as a teenager. You have it all—the sweetness, the nurturing qualities, the tenderness. But you're always thinking like a body-guard."

"I *am* a bodyguard."

"But the body you're guarding is yours. And we want this guy to find it."

"No, we don't. We just want him to find me appealing enough to come away with me for a week."

Becky rolled her eyes. "And you don't think your body will have anything to do with that?"

"I just don't want him to think I bought him for a week of sex, you know? Or I'll have more trouble than I'll know what to do with."

"He'll want to think that's why you bought him, whatever your reasons are. Now, come on. Where's your hair clip? I swear, I've never known a woman who carries one around so faithfully and never wears it."

"I want my hair to look neat," she said, watching Becky rout through the jeans Meg had tossed onto the bed. "But the clip always bothers me after a while, so I take it out." She caught her hair at the back of her head and held it there as Becky applied the filigreed clip.

Becky stood beside her and frowned into the mirror. "Earrings," she said, then went to her jewelry box on the dresser. "Silver and turquoise. Where... are they? Ah!"

She handed Meg a pair of large chased silver buttons with a beadlike turquoise inset. "There you go. Now, you look like a page out of an Eddie Bauer catalog. What do you think?"

Becky was right. She looked like a woman who ran a Fortune 500 company Monday through Friday and on weekends frolicked on a ranch with a handsome man in plaid flannel.

But it was a lie. And she remembered what Boradino had said about Pike appreciating honesty in a woman.

"Do not look like that," Becky ordered, pulling several shirts out of her closet and tossing them onto the bed. She put an arm around Meg's shoulders and pointed to the mirror. "This is the real you, Meg. Not the woman who fell for Daniel because he was the first man to notice you. He wanted the vulnerable part of you, not the strong part. You want a man who'll appreciate all of you."

Meg spread her arms and blew out her breath in exasperation. "The problem is *I* don't know who I am. I like men, generally, but in our work with

Women in Transition we hear so much about the bad
ones. And when my other job is to protect people
from those out to harm them, you start to see everyone as a threat. So I tried to loosen up about that, fell
in love with Daniel, and look where that got me."

"Free in the nick of time, if you ask me," Becky
said without apology. "Where's your backbone? You
weren't the problem, he was."

"Becky." Meg put her hands on her friend's shoulders and squeezed gently, apologetically. "You realize what Daniel changing his mind might do to
Grandma Rooney's endowment to your program?"

Becky nodded philosophically. "I like to think
she'll listen to reason when you explain that Daniel
left *you*."

Meg gave her a little shake. "Reason? Becky,
we're talking about the woman who offered blue-chip
stock to Kenny Kaiser in high school so he'd take me
to the prom."

Becky smiled. "So, she's a little...wacky. When's
she due back?"

"Next week sometime."

Guinevere Rooney Ross, Meg's maternal grandmother, was currently in Africa buying art for a small
museum in northern California. She was in her early
eighties and in good physical health. But she suffered
from a form of age-related dementia that caused her
to confuse and sometimes connect unrelated facts until her reality existed on a separate plane from everyone else's.

For the past two years she'd pleaded with Meg to
spend less effort on Becky's program and more time

trying to find the right man. In her mind, a woman's happiness depended upon husband and family.

When Meg introduced her to Daniel and told her they were engaged, her grandmother had said that since Meg had done what she'd asked, she would do something for Meg. At Meg's request, she had promised a substantial donation to the Women in Transition Center Becky had been dreaming of building for years, a place where young women without guidance or those starting over for any reason could stay until they found employment and felt secure enough to be on their own again.

"I don't know, Becky." Meg checked her reflection in the mirror and smoothed the jumper's short skirt. "Grandma told me she wouldn't do it if I chickened out."

"But *he* chickened out."

"Do you have any idea how hard it'll be to make her understand the difference? Especially since he left with a woman fifteen years older than I am? She'll blame me. I know she will."

Becky put the shirts inside a black plastic suit bag. "He found her money more appealing." Then she giggled. "And he never could get over the plate-glass window episode."

Meg rolled her eyes. "I'm an Amazon with an inferiority complex."

"You're beautiful, Meg," Becky corrected her, handing her the bag. "Remember what we're always telling the women in the program. The past doesn't matter. It makes no difference who tells you you're stupid or you can't do it, or you're never going to make it, or it's more than you should try for. Everything you need to succeed is inside you. *You* have to believe in you.''

Meg nodded. ''I know that, Becky. I have faith in my ability to support myself, to make friends, to live a good life. I'm just not sure I'm destined for love and marriage.''

''That's ridiculous. Of course, you are.''

Meg decided there was little point in arguing. Becky would believe what she wanted to believe, and Meg knew what she knew. After so many years of frightening men away with her physical strength and dexterity, she'd attracted a man who'd walked away less than two weeks before the wedding.

''Well,'' she said, taking a last look at herself in the mirror. She did look far more confident than she felt. ''This week isn't about love and marriage, anyway. It's about making myself appealing enough to Amos Pike that he'll come away with me. Then, I suppose if I have to keep him locked in a room until the toy show, I can do that.''

''You won't have to,'' Becky said, walking her to the door. ''Trust me. And don't worry about the center. I'll just keep dreaming about it awhile longer.''

AMOS FOLLOWED the brightly lit streetlights down Main Street in Lightning Creek, Wyoming, population fifteen hundred and something, and looked around him in disbelief. Time had stopped. That was the only possible explanation. Everything he remembered was still here—the general store on the east side of the street, Ellie's Dress Shop, Western Savings and Loan, the post office.

Across the street was Reilly's Feed Store, Twyla's Tease 'n' Tweeze—wait. The beauty shop might have been called something else back then, but it had been there. The Main Street Grill. The aroma of barbecue drifted out to him and he had to stop and breathe in a deep gulp of it.

It was twenty-five years ago. He was nine years old.

He felt a little shudder deep inside him that recalled that time even more sharply than the old familiar storefronts. It had been dark then, too, and he'd been driven into Lightning Creek by Barbara, his caseworker.

Barbara had already been working with him a year when she'd brought him to Lost Springs Ranch for Boys, a few miles out of town. She'd been kind and done her best to be supportive, but she hadn't known what to do with him after a year of moving him from one grandmother to another, from aunt to aunt.

She'd pulled the car over right about where he stood now. He could remember staring at the floodlit statue of Wyoming's famous cowboy on a bucking bronco that dominated the town's center.

"Amos, please try to hear me this time," she'd said. "You have to start helping yourself now. I know what happened to your mom and dad was a terrible tragedy, and it's not something you can get over quickly—even a smart, strong boy like you. But you have to make a start. You have to decide you want to go on. You can't keep running away and doing things that you know will get you hurt. That radio tower thing, Amos, was crazy! If you had fallen, they wouldn't have found enough of you to bury. Now, I know that sounds harsh, but it's time you…''

He could probably remember the rest of it if he put his mind to it, but he had finally found his footing here after a few rough months, and what had gone before was put away somewhere inside him with the memories of the parents he'd loved so much and had wanted so desperately to join.

It was surprising—and also humbling—to discover that despite all his hard work and success, he could still feel the loneliness that had swamped the little boy he'd been.

He pushed his way into the café, needing coffee. The square room was quietly lit to take advantage of the stone fireplace on one side. Booths lined the walls and tables and chairs were grouped in the center.

A score of tempting aromas mingled with that of barbecue, filling the air with a welcoming familiarity. Red meat had been considered a man-builder when Amos had been a boy, and the Lost Springs residents had eaten well.

When he'd been a young teenager, he and Bill Bartell, another resident of the ranch, would ride their bikes to town to spend the money they'd earned chopping wood for old Mr. Ferris, whose property had bordered the ranch. They would never miss treating themselves to a burger, fries and Coke at the café. While they ate, they would boast about their dreams for the future.

"I'm going to be a country-western star with babes following me everywhere I go," Bill would say.

Amos had envied Bill's single-mindedness. "I don't know what I'm going to do," Amos would say. "Be an architect, maybe. Something like that. And I'm gonna get rich. Yeah. Really rich."

Like Bill's dreams of stage-door babes, Amos had been sure that success in business would mean the company of women. And as a fifteen-year-old boy with raging hormones, he'd been convinced that would make up for being alone in the world. He just needed women.

The court had emancipated him at seventeen so that he could go east to college on a scholarship. He'd earned his degree in psychology with a minor in engineering—an odd combination of interests that had served him well when he turned his fascination with toys into a business.

In the years since then, he'd made friends, money and love to a number of women, but the heart of him still felt disconnected from the rest of the world. Set apart. Lonely.

The sound of country-western music and the buzz of conversation punctuated by loud laughter brought him back to the moment. He headed for the counter when he heard a voice call out from behind him.

"Pike?"

He turned to find a tall man in jeans and a western shirt standing by a table in the middle of the room, a cautious grin on his face.

"You are Amos Pike?" the man asked. Everyone was staring at him, women particularly.

It took Amos a minute to connect the tall, broad-shouldered man with an air of celebrity to Bill Bartell, the childhood friend with whom he'd shared hamburgers and dreams of the future.

Laughing, Amos changed direction and walked into his old friend's back-slapping embrace.

"Hell!" Bill exclaimed, taking a step back to admire Amos's well-cut suit. "You *did* get rich, judging by the look of you."

"And you got famous. I saw your duet with Alan Jackson in the video for Farm Aid. I suppose you do have babes following you everywhere."

They sat down on opposite sides of the table. For the first time Amos noticed another man seated at a right angle to him.

"Well, Amos," the man said, his aristocratic features elusively familiar. "Cutter Brown. You and I had kitchen detail together one month, remember? We were fencing with the brooms and managed to break all the juice glasses."

Amos laughed again, remembering the incident clearly. "We were grounded for a week."

"Yeah. As I remember it, we spent most of the time under the big table in the laundry room playing Lego."

Amos remembered that. The smells of detergent and fabric softener had made it an unusually sweet-smelling construction site. "What are you doing now?"

"I'm a developer," Cutter replied with a dry glance in Bill's direction. "Not the babe-magnet job our buddy has. I know you're the ultimate toy maker.

I read about you in *Forbes*. How'd you get into that?''

"Completely by accident. Titus Toys offered me an internship after college because I had a degree in psychology and they were planning to revamp their personnel tests and evaluations. One slow afternoon I was talking baseball stats with one of the designers, who happened to mention a problem he was having with the movement on an animated tiger. I helped him rework the structure, got a friend to help on the circuitry, and that was it. They transferred me to design.''

Bill raised a hand for the waitress. Amos ordered a burger and fries. His only concession to the intervening years was coffee rather than Coke.

"Well, I can't imagine you city slickers are going to make half the money in the sale barn that I am.'' Bill punctuated the boast with a tauntingly disdainful look at his companions. "I mean, you might look good in the society pages, but in the clinches, let's get real. Women want sex appeal and muscle. And you just don't find that in a three-piece suit.''

Cutter sent Amos a challenging look across the table. "We going to let him get away with that?''

Amos rolled his eyes. "He'll get set straight when we earn twice what he does. Poor man doesn't even know that women appreciate style and polish as well as muscle.''

"Probably because he's never had any,'' Cutter added.

"Yeah.''

Bill dug into an inside jacket pocket and produced

a hundred dollar bill. "This says you're wrong, and I earn a higher bid than either of you. Can you match it?"

Amos found two fifties and slapped them on top of Bill's hundred. Cutter wrote a check and added it to the pile.

"Who holds the bet?" Cutter asked.

Bill handed it to him. "Give it to Lindsay Duncan in the morning." Lindsay was the daughter of the man who'd founded Lost Springs Ranch for Boys and was its current owner. "Whoever wins donates it to the cause in his name. Deal?"

They mounded hands in the middle of the table as they used to do when they were boys.

"So." Cutter tucked the money into his pocket. "Nobody's been married?"

Amos and Bill shook their heads.

"Engaged?"

Two more noes.

Amos leaned back in his chair as the waitress arrived with their food. When she left again, he pounded out a blob of ketchup and passed the bottle to Bill. "How have you managed to avoid the groupies?"

Bill grinned slyly. "I don't avoid them entirely. The right one hasn't come looking for me yet."

Cutter frowned as he accepted the ketchup bottle. "Aren't you supposed to go looking for her?"

Bill shrugged. "Too busy rehearsing."

Cutter put the ketchup aside. "And you, Amos? I can't believe toys are more fun than women."

"They're not. But they're easier to deal with. I haven't found the right woman, either."

"And the right one would be?"

"Beautiful, amusing, nymphomaniacal—and a great cook." He dipped a french fry into the ketchup. "I'm sure she's just around the corner."

His companions laughed at his prerequisites, then sobered.

"She sounds perfect," Bill said.

Cutter nodded. "If we're lucky, she's a triplet."

LORD, IT WAS HOT. Meg, accustomed to breezy San Francisco, walked the grounds of the Lost Springs Ranch for Boys and looked around desperately for shade.

The place was filled with people. Children wielding water guns ran across the grass with barking dogs in pursuit. Meg would have welcomed a good soaking herself. There were booths and tables offering crafts for sale and advertising services. The air smelled of ribs and chicken grilling on an open pit, and something fresh and wild—some herb or grass she wasn't familiar with.

Her father looked up from a display of leather work, but except for a brief double-take at her appearance, he pretended not to notice her. He'd insisted on coming along to be certain everything went according to plan so that he could report back to Ms. Boradino.

Meg put her hands in the pockets of her jumper and walked on, liking the freedom and comfort of her short jumper—or, rather, Becky's short jumper—and her low-heeled white sandals.

She'd caught her hair back in the clip and put on the silver-and-turquoise earrings. Laboriously following directions in a magazine dedicated to glamour, she'd even made a serious effort with makeup. After receiving several second looks, she was feeling a little giddy with success.

Then she reminded herself that she had yet to meet her client, Amos Pike. As far as the Boradino plan was concerned, Pike's opinion was the only one that mattered.

A sudden attack of nervousness threatened to overtake Meg, and she headed for the shade of a spreading oak tree. She was immediately distracted by the sight of a beautiful quilt attached with clothespins to the tree's lower limbs.

A raffle table with tickets had been set up under the tree, and a banner proclaimed Converse County Hospital—35 Years of Sharing and Caring. Behind the table, a redhead with a bright smile looked up at Meg.

"Here to take a chance on a quilt or a bachelor?" she asked.

Meg handed her a ten-dollar bill. "Both. The quilt is gorgeous. I suppose the men are, too."

The woman handed her ten tickets. "You mean you haven't seen them yet?"

"No." Meg slipped the tickets into her purse.

"Well, here. Somebody left a catalog." A glossy folder was slipped under Meg's nose. On the cover was a picture of the ranch and bold letters that read

Bachelor Auction. "You'd better hurry if you're going to pick one out. They'll be starting in a few minutes."

Meg straightened and looked at the photos and accompanying bios, pretending a casual perusal. At last she found Amos Pike. And gasped.

"Aha!" The woman laughed. "You found one. I'm Twyla McCabe, by the way."

Meg tore her eyes from the brochure and shook Twyla's hand. "Meg Loria," she said.

Twyla shooed her toward the deeper shade. "You're looking a little flushed. You know we redheads can't tolerate too much sun."

Meg smiled and glanced once again at the photo of Amos Pike. She felt the same emotional punch to the gut she'd experienced a moment ago when she'd seen it for the first time.

She knew this man!

Oh, no one had ever introduced them, but he had Kevin Costner eyes and a George Strait smile, and she'd dreamed about him since she was twelve and the boy next door had called her a scrawny geek and told her she was too puny to grow boobs.

She'd have loved to find him to prove to him that he'd been wrong. But he hadn't been *that* wrong, so she'd never made the effort.

"Lord," she whispered to herself. "Look at him."

He'd been photographed in a tux, dark hair sideparted and neat, eyebrows dark slashes on a broad brow, nose nicely shaped. His jaw was strong, but his smile softened it.

Her pulse began to accelerate. She had to appeal to

this man, who probably had every heiress in the country and several international ones clamoring for his
attention. She couldn't do it. She simply couldn't do
it. She would have to find her father and explain that
this just wasn't...

"Favorite Song," the bio read, "'All for Love,' by
Bryan Adams. Best Come-on—'May I have this
dance?' Biggest Achievement—'The smiles on children's faces.'"

Okay, maybe she *could* do it. If this bio was true,
they were made for each other. He sounded like everything she'd ever wanted—and maybe a few things
she hadn't thought of.

Twyla came to put a hand on her arm. "Are you
all right?" she asked in concern. "Is the heat getting
to you?" She looked at the page Meg was studying,
then up into her eyes. "Or is it the man?"

Meg noticed that people, women particularly, were
streaming toward an arena a small distance away. A
stage had been set up and a long line of men was
climbing onto it.

Twyla patted Meg on the back and offered her half
a cup of lemonade. "Here. It's getting a little warm,
but the sugar might help. There you go. You don't
have to bid on him, you know, then you won't have
to deal with him."

Meg didn't bother to explain that she *wanted* to
deal with him. She just didn't know what to do if he
didn't want to deal with her. And she wasn't talking
about the Boradino plan.

She downed all the lemonade and felt the sugar
kick in almost immediately. *Get it together, Loria,*

she told herself as she handed back the cup. Amos Pike was a job, and she had to be in top form to carry it out. He might be her dream lover, but she could damn well bet she wasn't his. She would just have to get over it.

After slipping the catalog into her purse, she smiled at Twyla. "Thank you," she said. "I think you just saved me from heat prostration."

Twyla squeezed her arm. "Good luck in the raffle—and with your bachelor."

Meg strode toward the arena, putting on the persona of a rich and privileged woman out for a lark. This part she knew she could do. She'd been donning personalities to see how they fit since that day when she was twelve and would have given anything to be small and blond with a budding bosom.

Women crowded the rows of bleachers that had been set up in front of the stage. Meg pushed her way to the front and found a spot between a leggy blonde in a leopard sheath and a middle-aged woman in shorts and high heels.

Not all of the bachelors were on the stage, but she immediately picked out Amos Pike. In the flesh he was even handsomer than in his photograph. He was wearing the tux in which he'd been photographed, except that the heat had forced him to remove the jacket. It was tucked beneath one arm, and in the other he held the eighteen-inch-long plush polar bear, also in a tux, that was the trademark of his toy company.

Pike had undone the tie and the top button of the shirt, and he looked ready for action.

AMOS WAS A LITTLE surprised to find himself getting into this. Not that it was any less grisly than he'd imagined. The rowdy mob of women was cheering, whistling and hooting with easily as much enthusiasm as he'd have expected from their male counterparts if the roles had been reversed.

Except the roles never would be reversed in quite this way, he realized with a private smile. If men ever lined up a group of women on a dais and bid on them for a weekend's services of any kind, there would be a hue and cry among feminists from Boston to Los Angeles, and the men would be up on charges.

Relax, he told himself as he watched Rob Carter, now a doctor, be auctioned off for a considerable amount of money. *Don't lose your sense of humor. This is all in fun. And all for the ranch.*

It seemed only a matter of minutes before Amos took his place near the auctioneer. He turned in the direction of a few screams from the audience and smiled. The screams swelled to one loud, high-pitched, suggestive wail, and the front row of women leaned closer to the stage.

The auctioneer introduced Amos and explained that he was a toy manufacturer, repeating most of the information already in the auction catalog.

"All right, ladies," he began. "What am I bid for a man who obviously knows how to play?"

Another raucous cheer rose from the women, and Amos tossed the Pike's Pickled Pepper Toy Company bear into their midst. Grasping arms flailed the air for it, and the hapless bear disappeared within a flurry of tanned limbs, colorful coiffures and bright cotton prints.

Bidding began.

Please, God, he prayed silently as he smiled at the crowd. *Let me bring in at least as much as the bake-sale booth.*

Numbers were shouted quickly from one side of the crowd to the other.

No, Amos thought. He must be hearing things.

"Five thousand dollars!"

The bid came loud and clear—and in a disturbingly familiar voice. He turned in the direction from which it had come and picked Jillian Chambers out of the crowd.

She waved at him and blew him a kiss.

He was careful not to let the contempt he felt for her show on his face. He turned to the other side of the audience from where spirited bidding had also come and hoped for a counter bid.

A leggy redhead stood up in the front row, holding the stuffed bear he'd thrown. Blue eyes met his across the small space that separated them. She looked serious and just a little scared.

But she shouted firmly, "Six thousand!"

Jillian upped the bid another five hundred. Even the guys behind him were applauding.

"Seven thousand!" the redhead said.

"Seven thousand dollars!" the auctioneer repeated, turning to point at Jillian. "She's getting your man, little lady! Seven thousand dollars. Do I hear eight?"

Jillian obliged.

There was a long, pulsing silence. The cloudless

sky seemed to close in on them, the sun beat down and heat waves rippled over the landscape.

Amos began to make plans to buy himself out of whatever it was Jillian had in mind.

Then the redhead came a little closer, the bear clutched in her arms, her eyes still riveted on his. He waited with everyone else, unable to guess what she would do.

That fear in her eyes was mystifying, but the determination—particularly when it seemed to be aimed directly at him—was a decided turn-on.

"Ten...thousand...dollars!" she said, still staring at him.

The crowd went wild. The auctioneer went wild. Out of the corner of his eye Amos saw Lindsay Duncan jump up and down, then throw herself into the arms of Rex Trowbridge, the ranch's director.

Women leaned back to clear a path as Jillian stormed down from the bleachers and marched away.

Reckless with relief, Amos leaped off the stage, took the redhead into his arms and kissed her.

THIS IS GOOD, Meg told herself.

No. There had to be a better word than *good*. But she couldn't think of one because her brain wasn't working. Her lungs didn't seem to be functioning, either. And as the kiss went on one protracted moment longer, her knees lost their ability to function.

In some distant corner of her mind, she heard shouting and cheering, but all she was really aware of was the warm mouth on hers, drawing up from deep inside her the woman she'd always wanted to be—the woman she'd always known lived inside her, somewhere.

I did it! she thought as he finally raised his head and looked into her eyes. *I got him!*

She felt herself reeled into the warm, sexy depths of his hazel eyes and realized that that had been the easy part. Now she had to hold him for a week.

She let her forehead thunk against his shoulder. The crowd, already charmed by his flying leap off the stage, seemed to think her reaction was understandable.

The auctioneer pointed them toward the table where the auction officials waited. "Pay up, little lady."

Meg was grateful for Amos's supporting arm as she headed off to pay for him. She was in trouble—in more ways than one. The budget Boradino had given her was *five* thousand dollars.

CHAPTER THREE

"THERE YOU GO." Meg handed over the check with a cheerful flourish, as though she paid ten thousand dollars for a man all the time.

And as though she actually had that much in her account.

Her father would cover it for her, she knew, because with her customary attention to detail, they'd planned for just such a contingency. She would worry later about where the extra five thousand dollars would come from to pay him back.

Amos waited for her, hands in his pockets, weight resting on one leg. For an instant, she couldn't believe her own reality. Her mouth still tingled from his kiss, and though she knew he'd done it mostly to play to the crowd, it was one of the most amazing experiences of her life.

Suddenly she felt as if her life were in as much danger as his.

Hooking an arm in his, her woman-of-wealth-and-style persona in place, she led him toward the parking lot. "I should explain why I bought you," she said.

He smiled down at her. "Tell me it's because you need a sex slave for the weekend."

She waved that notion away with the bear she still

held in her free arm. "Oh, I've already had one of those and I dismissed him."

He frowned. "Unsatisfactory?"

She shook her head. "Actually, I need you for romance, not sex."

"Aw." A small smile accompanied the sound of disappointment. "Are you sure?"

He was teasing her, of course. Playing the role. She couldn't object to that. She was playing a role herself.

She pointed to the red Jeep she'd rented for the trip into the mountains. "Positive. I teach a class at a community college for women in transition. You know—women leaving bad relationships to start over, widows learning to cope on their own, young single women dealing with the world alone for the first time."

She unlocked the truck with the remote and climbed in behind the wheel as he got into the passenger side. They buckled seat belts and she put the key in the ignition.

"We talk about all the things they'll need to know—budgeting, cooking, child care, self-defense, but the one skill that's hard to teach or learn through practice is...how to meet kind, caring men who'll be an asset to their lives rather than a detriment."

As she turned the key, the engine came to life. She felt pleased with herself. Everything she'd said had been true—and with luck would draw him into the part of her plan that wasn't.

He looked puzzled but interested. "You didn't pay ten thousand dollars for me to be a sort of Show and Tell in this program?"

She pulled out of the parking lot and onto the road to Lightning Creek. "I bought you to be a sort of one-on-one classroom for me, so that I can go back to my students full of current and reliable information."

That didn't sound quite as convincing because she was now slipping into the lie part, but though he still looked puzzled, he didn't seem suspicious.

"I see...I think. But what makes you so sure I'm the kind and caring type?"

"You're in the paper all the time with one socialite or another," she replied, cranking up her enthusiasm a notch as the impossibility of the whole thing tried to claim her attention. She reminded herself that she'd gotten this far—something she hadn't been certain would ever happen just this morning. "And they always talk about what good company you are." Boradino had passed on this information. "So, you have everything the women in my class are looking for. You know how to treat women, you obviously love children if you're in the toy business, and you're a success."

He had turned in his seat to look at her. She pretended it didn't make her nervous.

"If you know that's what women want, why do you need me?"

"To pick your brain," she said. "Some of these women are making choices for the first time. Some have already made bad choices that they're still paying for. I'd like you to let me observe you, talk to you—for my class notes, of course—so that I can tell my students what to look for, and what the right man is looking for in a woman.''

He was watching her. She kept her attention on the road. If he *was* doubting her story, she didn't want to see that in his eyes. She had to get him to the mountain cabin, then he could doubt her all he wanted. By then, she could lock him up if she had to.

"And where are we doing this?" he asked.

All right. This was it.

She slanted him a winning smile. "I happen to have an entire week off and a cabin my family owns in the Bighorn Mountains. Do you have anything going on this week that can't be put off until next week?''

"No, I don't.''

Meg was shocked. It could not be that easy. She'd expected questions, arguments, the need to cajole him.

"You're sure?" she asked. "I mean…do you want to call your office or anything?"

"I'll do that from town. But unless you want to conduct a week of interviews with me in this tuxedo, we'd better pick up my things at the Starlite Motel.''

She glanced at him again.

He was smiling and looking completely relaxed.

Fear fled and her confidence rose a notch. All *right*. The Boradino plan was under way.

AMOS THOUGHT THERE WAS nothing quite as beautiful as the Wyoming countryside where the Great Plains met the Rocky Mountains. He seldom had the luxury of enjoying the scenery when he traveled. Even in a limo, with someone else driving, he was usually working in the back.

He could get used to this—being driven to an unknown destination by an attractive woman—though he wasn't entirely sure *why* he was doing it. For the sake of the ranch, of course. But he couldn't dispel the feeling there was something else at work here.

The obvious conclusion was that Meg Loria wanted a man for a week and hoped that a rustic setting and the considerable price she'd paid for him might encourage Amos to be grateful in a physical way.

But he didn't think that was it. Meg had an air of glossy sophistication, but he'd wager it didn't run too deep. He'd known many sophisticated women since he'd become in demand at parties and social events, and none of them had that nervous edge she had. Either she was lying about why she'd "bought" him, or she was beginning to regret having done it.

If she *was* lying, he was interested in finding out the truth. But if it was regret she was feeling, he intended to erase it for her. Because she was the most intriguing diversion from work and the general dullness of his life that he'd experienced in a long time.

She'd gone to gas up the car while he'd collected his things at the motel and called his office. He'd known Jeannette would be there, even on a Saturday. His assistant had taken the news of his departure for a week with her usual equanimity.

"We'll be fine," she'd said. "Everything's ready for the toy show, and the staff and I can even set up the display, so that you don't have to be there until the opening next Saturday morning."

"You make me feel superfluous, Jeannette."

"Hardly superfluous, Amos," she'd countered. "It's just that your work is done—at least for the toy show. We'll handle the rest of it. Did you bring in big money?"

He told her what had happened.

It sounded as though she'd choked.

"Jeannette?"

"Ten thousand dollars," she breathed in apparent astonishment.

"You don't think I'm worth it?"

There'd been a momentary silence, then he'd heard her draw a breath. "Every penny."

"Jillian was bidding against her. That drove up my price."

"Jillian," she said worriedly. "Amos, please be careful."

"Don't worry. I've been taking care of myself for a long time, Jeannette."

"So…where is she taking you?"

"Somewhere in the Bighorn Mountains. I'll be in touch. And I've got my cell phone if you decide you *do* need me for something."

"At that price," she said, "it sounds as though whoever bought you really needs you."

He'd had to agree with that. He'd said goodbye and hung up, thinking this week was bound to prove interesting.

"This is probably a rude question," he admitted now, turning in his seat belt to reach for a red spiral of hair that cascaded down the back of her neck from one long clip, "but is that color natural? It seems to fall somewhere between carrot and garnet."

She put a hand to her hair, seemingly surprised that he'd noticed it. "You don't think I'd dye it this color?" She laughed. "I can't wear anything from pink to burgundy. Supposedly redheads can wear red these days, but not this one. I end up looking like an apple with a tomato face."

He laughed at her description—and the suggestion that she'd ever be mistaken for produce. "I think it's very dramatic. It brings to mind fire, good wine, precious stones."

"Mmm." She concentrated on the road. "That's an appealing prospect—sitting in front of a fire, sipping wine and being presented with an expensive ring. I like it. My mother was a redhead."

She smiled a little wistfully at the road.

"She's gone?" he asked gently.

She nodded. "When I was about ten. She saw me off to school one morning, but she wasn't there when I got home. She'd had a coronary."

MEG FELT A LIGHT TUG on the curl Amos toyed with. "I'm sorry," he said.

When she glanced over at him quickly, she saw genuine sympathy in his eyes. She noticed other things, too. He had changed into cotton slacks and a light blue camp shirt, and looked even more gorgeous than he had in the tux.

"Thank you," she said, "but I adjusted pretty much. I still had my father and three older brothers, and they all closed ranks around me to make sure I had everything I needed."

"I imagine it was hard for men to make up for what a mother would provide."

She was a little surprised that he understood that. Then she remembered where and why she'd met him in the first place.

"Something similar must have happened to you," she said with another glance at him, "if you ended up at the ranch."

"Yeah. Light plane accident. My parents were celebrating their tenth anniversary with a trip to Reno in a friend's plane. They never got there."

Remembering the desperation she'd felt at her mother's death, she couldn't imagine what it would have been like had she lost both parents. "No siblings?" she asked.

He shook his head. "Just me."

"How old were you?"

"Eight. I spent the first year trying to join them. I used up the patience of every relative who tried to help me. One day I climbed a radio tower, determined to jump from the very top. Somebody saw me, called the police, and a couple of firemen brought me down. I ended up before a judge for that one, and he sent me to the ranch. It took me a while, but I finally found a sense of belonging there that helped me get over my death wish."

She looked at him in amazement. "I'm not sure I'd be tough enough to survive that much heartbreak."

He shrugged. "I kept trying *not* to survive, but somehow I did. Once I met kids who were at the ranch because their parents *chose* not to keep them, I realized there were others worse off than I. Feeling the emptiness of being alone in the world and knowing it didn't *have* to be that way had to be worse than being an orphan. So I finally got it together.''

"I'll say. Isn't Pike's a Fortune 500 company?"

"It was this morning." He grinned. "In today's market, that can change in an afternoon. Does being fed come with having my brain candled?"

She blinked at him. "Candled?"

"It's an old poultry farmer's term," he explained. "Before there were more scientific ways to determine the quality of an egg, the farmer held it up to a candle that allowed him to see through the shell to the inside and grade the egg. Like you do when you pick somebody's brain."

"Oh. And when were you an old poultry farmer?"

"I worked for one as a teenager. Now, about food…"

She pointed ahead. "There's a restaurant in Sweet Grass."

"Good." He sounded relieved. "I should have warned you that I have a large appetite."

"Oh?" she teased. "That must have been conveniently left out of your bio. As long as what you eat can come out of a can, we should get along fine. I stick to things that just have to be reheated."

"We'll have to do something about that."

"No," she disagreed. "I like it that way just fine. I don't like to cook. I don't mind reheating, but I don't like to actually have to chop and sear and steam and stuff like that."

"How did you get away with that in a house filled with men?" he asked. "I thought they'd have looked to you as the cook-housekeeper."

She shook her head. "My father hired one. And I was never really interested in domesticity, so he let me do my own thing."

He rippled an eyebrow in perplexity. "Then how come you're teaching a class in budgeting, cooking and child care?"

That was a good question. She'd gotten into it from the martial arts angle, and Becky had charmed and coerced her into the rest of it. But it would probably be better if he didn't know that. She didn't want him to doubt that her purpose for this week was anything but what she'd told him. And she could stay close enough to the truth without having to mention her self-defense skills.

"I have book knowledge on all those subjects," she replied with a smile. "I got involved because the class is run by a friend of mine who's doing it practically without funding. So I'm a volunteer."

"Do you have children?" he asked.

"No. Why?"

"I was just wondering if book knowledge on child care works."

"Well...sure it does. Most of the books are written by experts. Do you have children?"

"No."

"But you make toys for them without having any yourself. There's probably a similar principle at work."

"But I study the children firsthand. Twice a year

my staff bring their children in for a day, and we test
our new designs on them. It's amazing what little fingers can pull apart in two minutes. Or the simple
things that can entertain them for hours while some
of the complex things with all the bells and whistles
leave them cold. They seldom react in ways I expect.''

Most of Meg's friends now had children, and her
own lack of experience had become a sore spot with
her. The lost opportunity to have children was one of
the only reasons she could think of for missing Daniel. ''A lot of our women bring their children to class
because they can't afford child care. So I do have an
opportunity to observe children. And I do it more than
twice a year.''

That had sounded testy and she regretted it immediately. She decided she could afford to be honest
on that score. ''Children are sometimes a sore spot
with single women. I'm sorry. I didn't mean to snap.''

''It's all right. I'm not that sensitive. Anyway, I
wasn't challenging you, it was a genuine question.''
He pointed to the Sweet Grass city limits sign. ''Keep
your eyes open. You know, I'm starting to miss seafood.''

She laughed lightly. ''Me, too. But I doubt we'll
find any in the middle of Wyoming.''

''Anything will do.''

And then, just as the sun began to slip behind the
mountains, they came upon the Corral, which promised a prime rib for $9.99. Meg pulled into a parking
lot filled with pickups, RVs and sports utility vehicles.
''Serious cowboy country,'' she guessed.

"Looks like it." He climbed out of the car, and by the time she had put her keys in her purse, he was there to help her out. "You never mentioned where you live," he said as they walked side by side toward the restaurant.

She braced herself. He was going to think this was suspicious. "I'm from San Francisco," she said, then smiled into the surprise in his eyes as he opened the door for her. "That was part of the reason I picked you out of the catalog. The whole bachelor auction thing is kind of outrageous, you know, but it gave me a sense of familiarity, of having something in common with you."

He digested that with a mild frown. "No kidding."

"No kidding. Whoa." Meg stopped short two steps inside the restaurant. The prime rib special must have attracted every male in a ten-mile radius. She saw a sea of chambray shirts, and cowboy hats on tabletops, hooked on the backs of chairs and covering every peg on the wall, and at least thirty pairs of eyes giving her the once-over. They weren't necessarily disrespectful, but that much male attention from a woman who was unused to it made her take a step backward. There were only two other women in the room—the waitresses.

Amos bumped into her from behind.

"What's the...?" he began, then saw the staring eyes and put an arm around her shoulder. "They're just admiring you. They can't help it. It's instinctive." He pointed to an empty table across the room. "If you were alone, you might be in trouble. But you're not." He pushed her lightly down the narrow path between tables. "Go on. I'm right behind you."

Dinner, Meg thought, was a strange experience. From the moment Amos had agreed to come with her for the week, she'd felt in control of the situation. That was necessary in her line of work. But that sea of male faces had turned everything around. She might have been physically able to protect herself against them, but that wasn't the problem here. No one intended her physical harm, they just enjoyed looking, something that made her very uncomfortable.

In the name of some guy code, because Amos was with her, the men had finally turned back to their dinners.

Amos ordered the prime rib and Meg made do with a salad as she tried to reestablish her sense of security in the situation.

"Do you fish?" she asked, peppering her salad. "That's one way we can eat seafood—well, lake trout at least—at the cabin. It's on a lake."

He nodded. "Did some fishing at the ranch, but not much since then. The possibility of having trout for dinner one night, though, might make me brush up on my skills. You fish?"

"I know all the basics," she admitted. "The fish just don't seem to want to take my bait."

He grinned at her across the table. "Well, they must all be female fish."

To her complete horror, she felt herself blush.

He raised an eyebrow in surprise.

Every man in the room, as though tuned in to another man's successes, glanced their way and smiled or nodded as though Amos must have said something worthy of their silent congratulations.

"You're not used to being complimented," Amos observed, filling up her coffee cup from a carafe in the middle of the table. "Why is that?"

She rolled her eyes. "I lived with three brothers. Then I was engaged to a man who never really..." She pleated her paper napkin. "Daniel was more... cerebral."

"Was?"

"Was. He's gone. Broken engagement." She sipped at her coffee, hoping to discourage further discussion.

"Recently?" he asked. "You frown when you say his name."

"Just a few days ago, actually." She surprised herself when she giggled. It had all seemed tragic at the time, but today it was making her laugh.

He shook his head in amused disbelief. "I take it you're not brokenhearted over the loss. I think you're smart. I'd be suspicious of a man who was 'cerebral' where women are concerned."

"I hope the fact that it's so recent doesn't frighten you," she said, suddenly serious.

He negated that possibility with a shake of his head. "Nothing frightens me. Why?"

"I thought you might think..." She hesitated, wishing she'd never taken the conversation in this direction. Explaining what she meant was embarrassing. And she couldn't decide if it related to the truth or the lie of the Boradino plan. She finally just swallowed and said it. "I was afraid you might think you were just a ten-thousand-dollar...rebound purchase."

He didn't react to that admission. He simply studied her levelly and asked, "Am I?"

For the first time, she wondered if he just might be. Maybe she'd bought him in response to some impulse deep down in her sex-deprived psyche. She immediately dismissed the idea. It hadn't been her decision to go to the auction in the first place.

"No," she said with conviction. "You're my one-on-one learning experience for my module on finding and appealing to the right man."

He studied her a moment longer, then smiled. "I don't know whether to be disappointed or pleased. Rebound relationships can be bad news, but at least there's a sexual potential there that the classroom thing doesn't have."

Panic. Now that she had his attention, she didn't know what to do with it. "We're only going to be together a week," she reminded him.

"That's true. But it's not as though we're going to be on opposite coasts when we separate. We both live in San Francisco. If we started something, it wouldn't have to end because the week was over."

Her guess was he might not even be talking to her once the week was over. Of course, that was presuming he found out what she was really doing here. If all went well, he wouldn't have to.

Who was she kidding? she asked herself with her next breath. When had everything ever gone well for her?

But he was looking at her with those fathomless

hicle and turned to Amos. "I don't like to have a finger shaken in my face."

He nodded and raised both hands placatingly. "I'll remember that. You were making that pretty clear when I walked out the door. One guy was already on the ground, and the other one was squealing like a pig. You looked like you knew what you were doing."

"I did."

He folded his arms and studied her skeptically. "I know some schools have become dangerous, but is it so bad that teachers are now trained like CIA agents?"

She had to find some way to explain away what he'd seen. She tried diversion first. "Actually, I'm an assassin," she said, hands on her hips. "But don't worry, you're not my target. I'm between jobs at the moment, and I'm just trying to keep busy for a week."

He didn't laugh.

"Okay," she relented. "I've had martial arts training. My father insisted on it. And I have to admit it's come in handy at school a few times when angry husbands have come looking for the wives who've left them."

He remained unconvinced. "You're sure you're *between* jobs?"

"What do you mean?" she asked calmly, though the severe expression on his face was inspiring panic.

"I mean," he replied, "that I have a suspicion someone hired you."

She did her best to keep all thought out of her head

so that nothing would show in her eyes. "Like who? For what? I thought *I'd* hired *you.*"

"Like Chayco Toys." He came intimidatingly close to her, hands in his pockets. "To keep me away from the toy show next weekend."

"What toy show?"

He looked deeply into her eyes. She stood still under his gaze, knowing he was looking for guilt and horribly afraid he would find it and misunderstand just what it was she felt guilty about.

"Did you buy me at the auction," he asked carefully, "in order to keep me from the show?"

"You're obviously suspicious of me." She stared back at him, regaining a small measure of confidence. "Would you believe me if I answered the question?"

His eyes wandered over her face. "Yes, I would, because despite that display of physical confidence and control, you're very different inside—more open and ingenuous. And I think you're as interested in how this week is going to go as I am. If you lie to me, it changes everything." That wasn't a threat, but a simple statement of fact.

She looked him in the eye, wondering how a simple security job had suddenly become more of a danger to her than to him. "I was not hired by Chayco Toys to keep you from the toy show."

She beeped the doors and pulled hers open. He caught her arm before she could slip inside. Placing a hand on the side of the roof, he effectively imprisoned her in the V of the open door.

"Kiss me," he said.

She blinked at him. "What?"

"Kiss me," he repeated. "You have a fascinating mouth. It smiles, laughs, twists, pouts, depending on what you're feeling. It'll tell me the truth."

"You just said you'd believe me..."

"Indulge me."

She continued to hold her ground—not because she wanted to, but because he'd probably expect that of a woman telling the truth.

"You're forgetting what happened to those two cowboys back there," she said on a warning note. "Because in a manner of speaking, you're pointing a finger at me."

He smiled. "You're forgetting that I told you I'm not afraid of anything, particularly you. At least, not as a physical threat. Now, are you going to kiss me?"

She couldn't let him win this one. Emotionally, he had her severely off balance. The only way she could hope to keep the upper hand so that she could protect him was to keep him as unsettled as she was.

She tossed her purse in the back of the Jeep beside the bear, then looped her arms loosely around his neck. "You ready?" she taunted.

He gave her a nod. "More than ready."

"While I don't have a lot of experience, I do have a lifetime's collection of emotions. This will probably be more than you're expecting."

"Then let's *have* it."

He lowered his head and Meg rose on tiptoe to meet his mouth. Despite her claims of inexperience, she surprised herself with the sudden rush of feeling that spiraled in her like a cyclone the moment their lips touched.

Yes! her emotions said greedily. *Mine! This must be mine!* Not only was the movement of his mouth on hers pleasurable and wonderful, but it was right! It was what she'd always, always wanted—what she had to have.

That accepted, she gave the kiss everything she had. They drew their mouths apart to drag in air, and she took advantage of the opportunity to plant little kisses along his throat to his ear, to nip his earlobe, then to drag her lips across his eyelids, over the line of his cheekbones and back to his mouth.

His heart pounded against hers. It felt almost as though their heartbeats had mingled and were doubling—tripling—the pace of all the workings of her body.

Then suddenly, abruptly, he thrust his hand through her hair and pulled her away from him. He hadn't expected her to surprise him, and he didn't look as though he were pleased that she had.

They were in terrible trouble and both of them knew it.

"I'm driving the rest of the way," he said decisively, taking her arm and walking her around the car to the passenger side door.

"But you don't know where the cabin is."

"You can direct me." He pushed her inside, protecting her head with his hand.

"But…"

"If you drive," he said, leaning in to hand her the seat belt, "I'll be free to touch you. On mountain roads in the dark, that wouldn't be a good idea."

"But I'll be free to touch you," she pointed out with some relish.

"Not if you value your life, you won't."

CHAPTER FOUR

AMOS DROVE THROUGH the darkness, headlights on high down the narrow road flanked by what were probably aspens, and wondered what in the hell was going on here. Or maybe he didn't really want to know.

He was completely captivated by this woman already, though he wasn't sure he believed anything she'd told him. He didn't think she was lying, precisely—he had faith in his theory about the honesty in her mouth and the depths of her eyes—but something about the week she'd promised him didn't ring true, and he didn't know what it was.

His guess was that she had some purpose in all this beyond what she'd told him. And though he never let himself be made a fool of if he had any choice in the matter, he was going along with her plans because he considered her worth taking the risk.

That didn't mean that if she did make a fool of him, he wouldn't make her pay.

"Why would Chayco Toys hire someone to keep you from the toy show?" she asked from her side of their bubble of darkness. "I mean, we're not talking about weapons of mass destruction, we're talking about *toys.*"

"Toys are big business," he explained, liking the lazy cadence of her voice. She sounded sleepy. "And Pike's has had the market's biggest money-making toy for the last four years in a row. Everyone's wondering what we're bringing to the show this year. The press has speculated about it—particularly since we've had a break-in at the office and a fire at the plant. Someone's determined to see that we don't get to the show, or that what we're taking to the show doesn't get there."

"Why do you think it's Chayco?"

"Because its CEO and I have a history."

"You mean a bad history?"

"No," he replied. "We had a relationship for a couple of months that was nice, but she was only after my plans for the space station, our featured toy this year. I ended the relationship."

"And you've been enemies ever since?"

"She claims not." He slowed as his headlights picked out a fork in the road and a series of signs.

"Take Bluebell Lake," she said. "The cabin's about five miles down the road. What do you mean, 'She claims not'?"

Amos made the turn slowly. This road was even narrower and darker than the one he'd turned off. "She insists she didn't mean to steal the prototype, that she was photographing my plans to try to develop a joint venture for us because she was working on something similar. She keeps leaving messages for me and turning up beside me at charity dinners. That was her this afternoon bidding against you."

There was a momentary silence. "She's very beautiful," Meg said. She didn't sound too pleased about it. He liked that.

"Well, she's not. Not inside, anyway. I can't tell you how grateful I was that you outbid her. I was already trying to figure out how to get myself out of it if she'd won."

"Why did you suspect me of being hired by Chayco," she asked, "when I was bidding for you *against* her?"

"Because it would have been a good trick. I wouldn't put it past her. And it never once occurred to me until I saw you handle the guys in the parking lot and realized you weren't just another beautiful socialite."

"But I am," she said, her voice suggesting she was smiling over the immodest claim. Then she yawned.

He didn't dare take his eyes off the road—what he could see of it—but he said with conviction, "You're not 'just another' anything."

She was asleep when he found the cabin. He left the headlights on and got out to check the name on the mailbox that sat halfway between the road and the cabin. The box was in the shape of a mallard and read Loria.

Amos looked around but could see very little. At a short distance he could hear the lapping of water. Ahead of him stood the cabin, its lines indistinct in the darkness.

He opened the passenger door and leaned into the car, giving Meg a small shake. "Meg," he said quietly. "We're here. Meg."

She stirred sleepily but didn't wake up.

He patted her cheek. "Meg! Wake up!" He was momentarily distracted by the silkiness of her skin and paused to run the pad of his thumb along her jaw.

Her eyelashes fluttered, then her eyes opened, and he could have sworn he saw lazy pleasure in them when she looked up at him. But it was gone in an instant as she sat up briskly and looked around.

"What happened?" she asked. "Flat tire? Are we lost?"

"No." He took her purse and the bear from the back and put them in her lap. "You should have more faith in me than that. We've reached the cabin. You have a key?"

"Oh. Sure." She delved into her purse and produced a brass ring with a half-dollar-size disk hanging from it and one key. "I'll do it. It sticks."

She swung her shapely legs out of the car, and they were visible to mid-thigh in the dark. She shivered a little as she stepped out, and he wrapped an arm around her instinctively, rubbing from shoulder to elbow as they walked to the cabin steps. She dug into her purse again and produced a small flashlight.

They walked up the steps and onto a porch, skirting a wood box near the front door. The bear tucked in her left hand, she inserted her key in the lock, and when it stuck as she'd predicted, she turned sideways, raised her arms and gave the door a bump with her hip. It opened.

He laughed. "Such talent."

"I know." She inclined her head in pretended modesty as she stepped into the cabin. "I appreciate it for the gift it is. Now, if the caretaker did his job, the electricity should be on.''

Amos heard the flip of a switch and a fairly large main room was bathed in light.

''Ah.'' Meg spread her arms as though to embrace it. ''I'm so glad to be here.''

With large green-and-cream-checked furniture, a flowered rocker and a big brown leather recliner, the place looked more like a country cottage than a fishing cabin at the lake. There was a stone fireplace that separated the front room from a kitchen that was almost the same size, and Meg pointed out four bedrooms and a bathroom off a corridor on the far side of the main room.

''You put on the coffee,'' Amos said. ''I'll get the bags.''

She flipped on the porch light to guide his steps.

''Which bedroom's yours?'' he called as he returned.

''The one in the back. You can have any of the other three.''

The chivalrous thing would have been to leave at least one free between them, but he didn't. He chose the room next to hers. Knowing she would be within arm's reach had its appeal. He dropped his bags on the bed in the room, which was decorated in burgundy, gold and gray. A wallpaper border in a bookshelf pattern trimmed the wainscoting at waist level.

He carried Meg's bag into a white-and-yellow room with ivy vines on the wallpaper and natural wicker furniture. On her bedside table was a portrait of Meg in a cap and gown, surrounded by a distinguished older man and three younger men ranging in ages somewhere between hers and Amos's. Her father and brothers, he guessed. Sharing the double frame was a portrait of a woman with short red hair and a smile reminiscent of Meg's. Her mother.

He enviously studied the picture of the family, wondering how it would feel to know that somewhere in the world were four other people to whom you were connected by blood. Not that blood ties were everything, but he remembered how special his had been.

Now everyone in his family was gone.

"Coffee's up!" Meg shouted.

Amos followed her voice into the kitchen. Red and yellow peppers in a random pattern dotted the wallpaper and marched near the ceiling in a bright border. Yellow woodwork set off the colors and the red-and-cream-checked curtains on the windows and under an old sink. "This is not what you expect to find in the wilds of Wyoming," he said, sitting opposite her at a small round table in the middle of the room.

She had opened a carton of peanut jumbles and offered him one. "Brian's wife, Jamie, likes to decorate as a hobby," she said. "And she *loves* to wallpaper. Stand still around her when she's in a frenzy and you're liable to find yourself booked and wearing a border."

"Booked?"

"I don't know. It has something to do with putting the sticky sides of the paper together after you've soaked it. Makes it stick better or something."

"I take it she does this papering without your help."

"She does. Jamie doesn't need help with anything. She's a lawyer and she still has energy to burn. I'm good at painting, though." She looked up at the tall cupboards painted yellow. A narrow inset in the doors had been covered with the pepper wallpaper. "I did this room. I was just noticing that it needs a touch up. I should do that while we're here. The leftover paint's in the garage."

Amos laughed at the wallpaper. "I should get some of that paper for my office." When she looked at him in puzzlement, he pointed out the obvious. "Pike's Pickled Pepper Toy Company? You *are* sleepy."

She nodded ruefully. "I am good for nothing once I start yawning. These cookies are about all we had in the cupboard. We'll have to go to town for groceries in the morning. Unless you'd like to go without me and let me sleep in?"

He shook his head. "How would I know to buy peanut jumble cookies if you're not with me?"

"Actually, these are Ben's favorites. He was here last. He's single but has more women than an Arab prince. I like chocolate-dipped shortbreads. Frank's a priest. Brian's the oldest, then Frank, then Ben, then me."

"A priest?" It was hard for him to imagine that the same sets of genes that had produced Meg's gorgeous legs and her ability to kiss had also made a man of the cloth.

"Yes. He's great. Teaches at a boys' school in east Los Angeles. Tough and holy. It's a powerful combination."

Amos watched her nibble at the cookie while she

talked. She seemed to be transforming from the sophisticated socialite who'd bid on him in the arena to
a woman suddenly more comfortable on her home
turf. Either she'd forgotten her "disguise" or it had
slipped off of its own accord. She beamed when she
talked about her family.

He reached for his coffee and put it to his mouth,
still watching her. The first swallow convinced him
he'd ingested bug spray—or puddle water—or gym-
sock stew. He emerged from the cup, coughing and
choking.

Meg ran around the table to slap his back. As his
coughs quieted, she pulled up a chair beside him and
waited worriedly for him to speak.

He drew the cup toward him and was surprised to
find that its contents even *looked* like gym-sock stew.
"What *is* that?" he asked in a strained voice. He
coughed again.

"Chamomile and rose-hip tea," she replied,
smoothing a lock of hair off his forehead.

He didn't know whether to be more shocked by her
touch or the fact that roses had hips. "It tastes..."
He struggled to find a gentle word and decided there
wasn't one. "Terrible," he finally said.

She took the complaint in stride. "I'm sorry. I always have it at night instead of coffee. Coffee'll keep
you awake."

He cupped her cheek in his hand. "Meg, when
you've been sold at auction, offered a week with a
beautiful woman who wants you for reasons that
aren't sexual, and you've driven many miles down

country roads in the pitch-black darkness, nothing would keep you awake.''

She giggled. "You have had quite a day, haven't you? Go on to bed. I want to make a grocery list for tomorrow.''

The idea of a bed sounded wonderful at the moment. A bed with *her* in it sounded like heaven. But he knew it was out of the question. He settled for a more reachable goal. "Do you want to kiss me good-night?''

"No," she replied with demoralizing speed and sincerity. "We're like oil and matches. I don't think it's a good idea.''

"But oil and matches produce favorable results," he argued reasonably. "Light, warmth…''

She eyed him with reproach. "You're trying to charm me.''

There was no point in denying it. "Is it working?''

"Yes, but no.''

He narrowed his gaze as he tried to interpret that answer.

"It means," she explained, "that I'm charmed, but I'm not kissing you good-night.''

"All right, then." He stood and carried his cup to the sink and poured its contents down the drain. "Of course, I'm not surprised that a woman who could brew something so vile would deprive the man of her dreams of a good-night kiss.''

He turned from the sink to find her standing, also. "How did you know," she asked, blue eyes wide, "that you're the man of my dreams?''

For an instant, he wasn't sure how to respond. "I,

uh, didn't know that I was. I just thought I'd work toward becoming…'' He stopped abruptly and smiled. ''I am? Are you sure?''

She wasn't going to answer him, he saw that instantly. She was mentally backpedaling, wondering how to get herself out of the predicament of having divulged that secret.

So. He was the man of her dreams. He felt power surge through his veins. ''Well,'' he said, keeping his distance but reaching out to pinch her chin. ''That's only fair, since you're the woman of mine. Good night.''

He left her standing in the middle of the kitchen, that expressive mouth hanging open.

He'd been wrong, though, about being able to go right to sleep.

AMOS FINALLY DRIFTED OFF as light became visible beyond the window. He thought he'd heard Meg talking during the night, then concluded she must have had the radio on. Later he'd listened to her bedsprings creak as she tossed and turned. He heard her get up a couple of times, and once he thought he'd heard her go out to the kitchen.

He wondered what had made her so restless. Too many peanut jumbles, possibly.

Screams woke him to brilliant daylight. It took him a minute to remember where he was—and why, in his lonely and solitary life, he heard a woman screaming.

Meg! He shot out of bed and raced to the kitchen. As he rounded the corner of the fireplace, he almost

collided with the business end of a broom being
wielded like a lance. He dodged it just before it would
have turned him into a sieve.

He caught the handle to which Meg was attached.
She wore a San Francisco Giants T-shirt and nothing
else. Her hair was loose and rumpled and her eyes
wide.

"Meg!" he shouted, catching her arm in one hand
and blocking the broom with the other. "What? What
is it?"

"Oh! Amos!" She threw an arm around his neck
and held on tight. "There's a rat in one of the bottom
cupboards!" Then she drew back and handed him the
broom. "Here."

"God," he said, feeling his pulse dribble back to
normal. "I thought it was rampaging bears at the very
least."

She looked defensive and then embarrassed.
"Sorry. Indiana Jones was afraid of snakes. I'm afraid
of rats. But you're not afraid of anything, right?
That's what you said!"

That's what he got for making extravagant claims.

"Which cupboard?" he asked, advancing into the
kitchen.

She followed behind him and pointed over his
shoulder to the one closest to the back door. It was
partially open and he could hear rustlings inside.

He opened the back door and left it ajar, then
opened the cupboard beside the one with the intrud-
ers, pulled out a few pots and pans and inserted the
broom.

A fat black-and-white body ran out. It was not a

rat at all but a raccoon, who didn't seem to understand why he wasn't welcome. *She,* Amos mentally amended as two smaller black-and-white bundles followed her out.

"Oh, no," Meg said regretfully, standing in the open doorway and watching them run away. "It was just a raccoon. With babies!"

"But how did she get in there?" Amos handed her the broom and leaned outside to investigate. He spotted a hole in the siding and concluded that it went through to the cupboard. "Is there a builder's supply in town?" he asked, drawing back into the kitchen. "I'm not a carpenter, but I can fix that so they can't get in again."

She continued to stare worriedly after the raccoons. "There is. But today's Sunday—they won't be open. We can go back to town just for that tomorrow. Remind me to get dog food for the raccoons." He was about to remind her that, though cute, raccoons were still a pest, when he realized that she stood only two feet away from him in nothing but a T-shirt, the nipples of her round, high breasts pushing at the fabric. He couldn't seem to form the words—or even remember them.

MEG KNEW SHE WAS STARING, but the only concession she could make to good manners was to raise her eyes from Amos's lean hips, which were covered in gray-blue boxers with the red-and-white Big Dog logo all over them, and keep her eyes on his chest.

It was broad and muscled and covered in the same gray-blue cotton. The fabric stretched across his ribs, clung to his flat stomach and disappeared into the shorts.

She was aware of long, strong legs below the boxers, but didn't dare look at them.

Air was at a premium.

She met his eyes. They were riveted on hers. Tension tightened between them, then he asked with a small smile, "How about a good-*morning* kiss?"

She considered that suggestion for one delicious moment, then remembered that this was serious. She was here to protect him, and she couldn't afford to be further distracted. She ignored the fact that she'd just run in terror from a raccoon.

"I'll get dressed," she said, and hurried away without looking back.

IN JEANS AND A STANFORD sweatshirt, Amos walked onto the front porch to wait for Meg—and was overtaken by the beauty of his surroundings.

About ten yards from the cabin, the lake stretched out, embroidered by the sunshine and taking its color from the bright blue sky. He guessed it to be a quarter of a mile across, its shoreline dotted with cabins and boat docks.

A small green rowboat bobbed at the end of a rope tied to the foot of the dock. The scene was so inviting that he wandered to the middle of the sturdy little pier and looked around him at the broad expanse of blue.

This was the perfect vacation spot. A man could endure whatever a year in the trenches of the corporate world demanded of him, if he knew he could come here in the summer to relax. Fishing in that little boat, evenings on the porch with a Bloody Mary and a woman beside him who'd made promises for the night. It would be paradise.

"You contemplating a swim," Meg asked, "or the proverbial long walk off a short pier?"

She came to stand beside him, wearing jeans and a silky white shirt. Her hair had been twisted into a coil and fastened to the back of her head with that toothy clip. She was like a sun catcher, holding and reflecting light.

"I was wondering," he replied, turning her toward the shore, "which one of us will be rowing when we go fishing."

She smiled at him as they walked over to opposite sides of the Jeep. "I have the strength to row," she said, climbing in behind the wheel. "Though I do have a tendency to row in a circle."

He laughed as he slipped in and pulled his door closed. "Not a good thing when you're trying to get to the middle of the lake where the fish are."

She gave him an innocent smile as she turned the key in the ignition. "So, maybe *you* should row."

She'd manipulated that nicely. "Cleverly done, Miss Loria," he said.

She laughed unashamedly. "I thought so."

THE TOWN OF BLUEBELL LAKE had twenty-three hundred full-time residents and a little downtown that was only one block long. It looked just as it must have in the days before Wyoming became a state. This morning, families in their Sunday best were pouring into a little white-steepled church at the end of the block.

Meg took him to a small bakery first, located in the bottom of a brick building on a boardwalk. "They're open on Sunday morning," she explained, "because they cater to the after-church crowd." They had a breakfast of apple fritters, orange juice and coffee.

They bought groceries in a very modern market at the other end of the block. It was small, but it had a deli counter, a gourmet section and every food product advertised on television.

"I can make spaghetti," Meg said as they pulled a cart from a lineup of about a dozen. "I'm good with salad, and I can make tacos. Does any of that appeal to you?"

"I like all those things." He took control of the cart. "But maybe since this week is supposed to be for you to learn about husband material, I should cook tonight."

She tried to take the cart back. "That'd be nice, but how many men really do cook? Most of my women won't be able to find one."

"True, but the cooking's not the point."

"It's not?"

"No. True devotion lies in giving of yourself, sharing your talents. And cooking's something I can do. Compliments and gifts are cheap, but working for your mate to do something special is husbandly—or wifely."

She let him have the cart. "You really do know how to do this."

"I do. Follow me."

An hour later they headed home with four bags of groceries and twenty pounds of dog food.

While Meg put out a bowl for the raccoons, Amos investigated the garage and found a board that would temporarily cover the hole in the siding.

She fixed a salad and sandwiches for lunch, then hauled the fishing gear out of the garage.

"Want to see if we're any good at this?" she asked, holding the rods out to him. "Do you have a hat?"

"Yes, I would," he replied, taking the tackle box from her, too. "And no, I don't."

"Okay. If you take that stuff to the boat, I'll meet you there in a minute."

She packed a small cooler with soft drinks and chocolate-dipped shortbreads, scooped up the CD player she kept in her bedroom and snatched one of Brian's baseball caps from the motley collection in the front bedroom. Then she ran down the dock toward the boat, happier than she'd been in ages.

She handed everything down to Amos, then lowered herself into the boat. Amos lifted her the last few feet and set her down in front of the thwart.

"Since you row in circles," he said, freeing the line that tied them to the dock, "I'll get us to the middle of the lake. But you have to do something to earn your keep, so catching dinner is up to you."

She took her seat. "I thought you bought a roasting chicken for dinner."

"I did. Which we'll have if you fail in your assigned task." He sat on the rowing thwart and took the oars. "I'm just giving you a choice." He pushed them away from the dock with the blade of an oar, positioned them expertly to head for the middle of the lake, then began to row with smooth, even strokes.

"Pardon me," she teased while trying to memorize his movements. He made it look so easy. "But that sounded more like applying pressure than offering a choice. And I don't think that's a good quality in a husband."

He grinned. "Probably why I'm still single."

Since it was still June, the summer anglers hadn't arrived yet. Even the local weekend fishermen were either still in church or otherwise occupied, because the middle of the lake was a sunny, peaceful spot.

A fragrant breeze stirred gently as Meg put on a military college baseball cap and flipped the bill back.

"That where you got your martial arts training?" Amos asked.

"No, I went to a dojo. All my brothers and I did. My father was mugged once and wanted us to be able to protect ourselves. This is Ben's hat, though."

"The one with as many women as an Arab prince."

"That's the one."

Amos studied the hat she'd brought for him. "USS *Kearsarge,*" he read, then put it on, pulling it down low over his forehead. "Whose is this?"

"Brian's."

"Father Frank wasn't a military man?"

She smiled as she opened the tackle box. "He's a Jesuit. They're considered the soldiers of Christ, so he has his own military career going."

Several moments later, lines in the water, they leaned back against their life preservers.

"Did you bring a cooler for the fish?" Amos asked.

"You're an optimist," she said. "No, I didn't. There's not enough room on this thing. In the summer when we're all coming and going, Dad brings up his forty-four-foot Tollycraft. This is Ben's. He hangs it in the garage in the winter, but he was here last week."

Meg turned on the disk player and adjusted the sound.

"You're going to scare the fish," Amos warned.

"I don't think so. The only time I caught anything, I was playing Trisha Yearwood. It's my theory that Wyoming fish respond to country-and-western music."

"You play it all the time?"

"Yeah."

He smiled with forbearance. "If you play country-and-western music all the time, but you've only caught one fish, doesn't that suggest that they *don't* generally respond to it?"

She rolled her eyes. "You could be related to my brothers. Logic doesn't rule everything, you know. Some things are instinctual."

"Really."

"Yes. And you should go with a woman's instinct, because our brains have more fibers connecting the left and right neocortex, and that makes it easier to blend intuition and logic."

"But you just said logic didn't matter."

"No, I said it didn't always rule. That's a different thing entirely."

"*You're* a different thing entirely."

"That's what Brian always…ah! I've got something! Amos, I've got something!"

He wedged the tip of his pole under the thwart and leaned up to be ready to help. "Okay. Take it easy. Don't hold too tight or he'll snap the line."

"You owe Trisha Yearwood an apology!" The fish pulled away and circled when he could pull no farther. Amos ducked as she guided the line over and around him as the fish came around the other side.

Meg cranked the reel and pulled lightly on the line. The fish did another turn, then just as Amos sat ready with the landing net, the line snapped and fell slack, and a ripple in the water moving like a torpedo marked the escape of a very happy trout.

Meg groaned and brought in what was left of her line.

"I'm sorry," Amos commiserated. "The line was probably weak from having sat in the garage all winter."

She made a wry face at him. "Our story is that the fish was bigger than the test of the line. Okay? A forty-pounder."

He swatted her shoulder with the net. "Or we could just say that you snagged Nessie."

"Very funny. I need a cookie."

"Me, too."

She reached for the cooler and made another face. "You didn't lose a fish. Why do you need a cookie?"

"I'm providing moral support. Depletes the sugar."

"Oh, right. 'We could just say you snagged Nessie' is providing moral support? Sounded like you were heaping scorn to me."

He winked at her. "Never. Logic doesn't always apply, remember? Some things are instinctual. Instinctively I knew you'd rather be teased than pampered."

She tossed him a cola. "You are *so* not correct." Then she held out the bag of cookies.

He put his pop down and snagged one. "Thank you. Well, I'll provide the pampering at dinner."

They'd listened to the entire Trisha Yearwood CD and were in the middle of a Dixie Chicks tune when Amos decided that he could spend the rest of his life right here—with Meg. She was as perfect for him as he'd thought she was the first time he saw her in the crowd of women at the auction.

He wasn't sure what the fear he sometimes saw in her eyes was all about, but it seemed to be abating now that they were here. She was more genuine than any woman he'd ever met, and what had begun yesterday as a fascination was now turning into something that seemed to need more room than his chest could provide.

He felt a ridiculous impulse to shout and hear the sound echo around the lake.

"Well, this is doing nothing," Meg said, reeling in her line and unhooking a brightly colored lure. She reached into the tackle box for something else.

Then she gasped in apparent pain and withdrew her hand from the box. A colorful fuzzy lure dangled from it, its hook embedded in the pad of her forefinger.

CHAPTER FIVE

MEG SLAMMED THE LID closed and rested the back of her injured hand on her knee as Amos reached out to draw her beside him onto the middle thwart.

"Great," she said in self-disgust. "Now you can use me for bait." She came to him on her knees, keeping her weight low and in the center of the boat. "How trite. Every one of my brothers has a fishhook story. I've always teased them about being careless."

Amos examined her finger and found that the barb was well stuck. "Is there a doctor in town?" he asked.

"No. The nearest doctor's in Sheridan. About forty miles."

He'd been afraid of that. He knew what he had to do and it wasn't for the fainthearted.

"Wire cutters in the tackle box?" he asked.

She nodded.

While he reached for it, she tugged at the hook, trying to back out the barb. "Ow! Ow! Ow!" she cried.

"Don't do that!" he snapped at her, catching her wrist to stop her.

"Well," she snapped back, "we're not driving forty miles to find a doctor we'll probably have to chase down on a Sunday. I have to get it out myself. Do you have a knife?''

"We don't need a knife." He put the wire cutters on the thwart beside him.

"We don't?''

"No. You've got me—class model for what to look for in a husband." He grinned as he caught her arm under his and flattened the back of her hand on his thigh. "He should be able to remove barbed fish-hooks. This happened to me when I was a kid and Mr. Duncan at the ranch got it out."

She was peering around his shoulder and he met her eyes apologetically. "But it hurts like hell," he warned.

She heaved a reluctant sigh. "It already hurts like hell. So, do it."

"Okay." He drew a breath to steady himself. "I have to push the barb through because it won't back out. Then I'll cut off the barb and withdraw the shaft."

He felt her slide down to rest her cheek against his back. "All right. You know, I thought about painting cupboards this afternoon instead of fishing, but I dragged you all the way out here and I didn't want you stuck in the cabin when there was sun on the lake and…''

Amos took advantage of her mild distraction to work quickly. With a firm, steady movement, he pushed the barb through, ignored her scream of pain and her fingernails in his back while he snipped off the curved end.

"Barb's off, almost done," he said, tossing the clippers aside and gently withdrawing the shaft.

MEG DIDN'T THINK she'd ever had anything hurt as much in her entire life. And that included a few punches and falls she'd taken in the line of duty.

White-hot pain pulsed in her hand for a long moment as Amos did his work. She held a fistful of the back of his shirt and ground it between her fingers while the pain persisted.

She knew the instant the shaft was free. Eighty percent of the pain abated.

Amos's arm came around her to pull her in front of him. He held her tightly. "I'm sorry," he said, kissing her forehead. "I know that was awful. You have a first-aid kit on the boat?"

She sank weakly against him, feeling considerably better but very grateful that he'd known what to do and that she now had him to lean on. "No kit on the boat. But there's one in the cabin."

"Is your tetanus shot current? Or do we have to chase that doctor down, anyway?"

"It's current." She straightened away from him and examined her bloody finger. "Whew! I need coffee."

"Lie down in the bow," he said, "and I'll get you home." He took a handkerchief from his pocket and wrapped it around her finger.

She saw as he worked that his fingers were also covered with her blood. She leaned wearily against her lifejacket and smiled at him as he began to row.

"Thank you. I'm sure that wasn't easy for you, either."

A quick glance of his hazel eyes told her he was as glad it was over as she was. "No, it wasn't. I need coffee, too. But it's all part of the expert-in-residence service."

He insisted she leave the gear in the boat, that he would come back for it, and carried her up to the cabin.

"You're playing the role to extremes," she protested, but looped her arms around his neck, anyway. It felt wonderful to lean her head on his shoulder and let him be responsible for as simple a task as walking. "I feel fine."

"There are no extremes in a lover's attentions," he corrected her. "Tell your ladies to look for a man who'll go the extra mile for her. Because that's what he's looking for in her."

"I will. And if you ever need to be carried anywhere, I'm there for you."

"That's a comfort. But maybe I'll put Xena, Warrior Princess, on standby, just in case."

"You're forgetting the parking lot again."

"I'm not likely to forget anything about you." He turned the knob on the front door, kicked the door wide, then sidled through to deposit her on the sofa. He pinched the clip out of her hair, combed his fingers through it, then eased her back against a pillow.

"I don't need to lie down. I'm perfectly…"

He pushed her back as she tried to rise, then pulled off her tennies. "Just relax. Where's the first-aid kit?"

"Bathroom. Bottom right-hand drawer."

He pointed a finger at her as he left the room. "Don't move."

Amos was back in a moment with a small bottle of alcohol, a tube of antibiotic cream and a wide bandage. The alcohol hurt almost as much as the hook had, and she groaned and tried to pull her hand away.

But he held it firmly, attempting to fan away the sting with his other hand.

It was over in a moment, and he applied the antibiotic, then the bandage.

He left again and returned with a bottle of aspirin from his room and a glass of water. "I'll put on a pot of coffee and get the gear. Stay down."

He took a cotton throw from the back of the sofa, opened it over her, then went into the kitchen.

Wallowing in his attention, she snuggled into the pillow and closed her eyes, intending to relax until the coffee was ready.

When she awoke again, the room was in shadow and filled with the most wonderful aromas drifting in from the kitchen. She sat up feeling headachy. She groaned and leaned sideways against the back of the sofa.

"Hi." Amos sat beside her and framed her face in his hands to assess her condition. "Feeling punk?"

"My head aches," she replied, her voice raspy. "That always happens to me when I nap." She held up her bandaged digit. "Finger feels better, though."

"Good." He brushed the hair out of her face and ran a thumb lightly over her cheekbone. "You feel like getting up, or you want me to bring you a cup of coffee?"

"I'll get up."

He stood and offered his hands to steady her as she swung her legs over the side of the sofa, then used him as a support to pull herself up. He pulled a chair out for her and poured her a cup of coffee. Its subtle hazelnut flavor went to work instantly, easing her out of her fuzzy state and back to life.

Amos opened the oven door and, with a tea towel folded in four, pulled out the rack on which a chicken roasted in a shallow pan. It was a light gold color and dotted with aromatic herbs. He spooned the drippings over it, then pushed the rack back in and closed the door.

On the stove was a rice mixture in the frying pan and something in the steamer. She remembered that they'd disagreed over broccoli versus cauliflower, and finally bought brussels sprouts.

"I'm beginning to think," she said, watching him move around the kitchen, lean hips in snug, worn jeans a pleasure to behold, "that I might be doing my ladies a disservice by using you as a class model."

He picked up his cup and turned to lean against the counter. "Why is that?" he asked.

"Because you're too perfect," she answered. "How many men out there can be doctor, nurse, chef and personal conveyance, all in the same afternoon?"

"You'd probably be surprised. And I do have a few bad habits."

"Like what?"

He gestured with his cup. "Well, I do the definitive thing with the remote."

"Oh, no."

"'Fraid so. I don't shave on weekends."

She raised an eyebrow. "May I point out that it's Sunday and you're shaven?"

"Yeah, but I'm being a class model."

"Oh, yes."

"Sometimes when I'm working on an idea, I'm locked up for days, just fiddling with it. Or I bring the design guys over and we stay with it till it's right."

She nodded. "Throes of creation. I can understand that."

"I'm occasionally short-tempered and grumpy."

"What makes you grumpy?"

He thought about that. "Being unable to figure out a design problem. Or any kind of problem, I guess. Being lied to."

Meg absorbed that bit of information with a barb that felt like the one that had been stuck in her finger. Then she dismissed it instantly from her thoughts so she didn't betray by look or action that that was precisely what she was doing here—lying to him.

"Well, that all sounds very normal," she said with a bright smile. "I don't imagine any woman would be put off by that confession. What are *you* looking for in a mate—besides honesty?" She added that last without a change of expression.

A pleat appeared between his brows. He shifted his weight and crossed one large Rockport over the other, the toe propped on the floor. "It sounds selfish when

I reel it out," he said candidly, "because I want a lot—humor, strength, a certain savvy, a few frailties..."

"Frailties?"

He grinned. "Yeah. I want to be able to feel that I can come to her rescue once in a while."

"Ah." Meg spread her hands out before her. "All she has to do is catch a fishhook in her finger."

He took a modest bow. "She has to want a couple of kids, a big dog, be able to put up with a workroom she can come into but never, ever clean."

"Is that it?"

"No." He maintained the serious expression, though she saw the glint of humor in his eyes. "I'd like her to wear black lace undies all the time, so that even when we were at a social function or if I were thousands of miles away on business, I'd know she had them on just for me."

"What if she doesn't like black lace?"

He shook his head regretfully. "Then she's out of the running."

"But there are so many beautiful colors in lingerie today," she argued, smiling. "You're being a little old-fashioned, there, Pike."

"Can't help it." The stove's timer beeped, and he stretched a hand back to turn off the burner under the rice. "When I was fourteen, the guys and I used to talk women in the dark, and the ultimate of all things seductive was black lace underwear. I had a lingerie ad taped to the inside of my footlocker."

Meg got up to get silverware as he turned back to the stove to put the finishing touches on dinner. "So any woman not in black lace panties is out as a prospective mate?'' She stood in the middle of the room, knives and forks in hand, and frowned. ''I don't think I'll tell my ladies that part.''

''Unless, of course, she's willing to be converted.'' He placed a platter with the golden chicken in the middle of the table, then the bowls of rice and brussels sprouts. ''Or can convert me.''

The silverware placed, she looked around for something else to do. ''Shall I pour coffee?''

''No.'' He walked around to her side of the table and pulled out her chair. ''I'll take it from here.'' She sat and he pushed in her chair. Then he retrieved a bottle of wine from the counter and two glasses.

''A prospective husband would serve wine for atmosphere,'' she asked as he poured, ''or seduction?''

He handed her a glass half-filled with white wine. ''For conversation,'' he replied, taking his own chair. ''He has to know something about the woman before he can plan a seduction. And seduction isn't what every woman needs, anyway.''

''Really? I thought men were all convinced that any woman would benefit from their lovemaking.''

He gave her a scolding look across the table. ''Now, how can you hope to help each of your women find the man she needs when you generalize about all of them? They're as different as women are.''

He held his glass toward hers in the middle of the table. She put her glass to it. ''To us,'' he said.

She drew her glass back an inch, feeling curiously, inexplicably in danger. "Us?"

He raised an eyebrow at her withdrawal. "I presume a teacher learns, then passes on what she teaches, am I right?"

"Yes."

"Well, that's what's going to have to happen here if you expect to get your ten thousand dollars' worth." He smiled into her openmouthed expression. "We're not talking seduction, remember? So there's no need to look so cornered. We're talking about getting to know each other—the foundation for any relationship."

He continued to hold his glass out toward her. A little reluctantly, she clinked hers against his. She had that in-over-her-head feeling again. She had to get over that.

And she had to remember that this whole scenario was about protecting *him*, not about protecting herself. So it was inevitable that keeping him here was going to involve making herself vulnerable to his perceptive observations. But the job was all-important—not only because the client was always Loria Security's priority, but because she had to prove to her father and brothers that she was as able to do the work as they were.

It had taken almost all of her strength to hold back her tears rather than let them fall when she'd told her family the wedding was off. She could still see the worried, protective looks on their faces and felt as though she'd somehow failed them. They'd wanted her to be happy and she wasn't. She was miserable.

But she wasn't miserable now. Now she was a little scared. Curiously, that seemed to be an improvement.

Amos carved two succulent slices of chicken and spooned up side dishes onto her plate, then served himself.

He lit a match to the two candles he'd placed in the middle of the table and turned off the overhead light. Meg found the atmosphere suddenly mellow.

"What led you to teaching?" he asked as they settled down to eat. He pushed a plate of rolls toward her. "And why teach adults and not children?"

"I had no intention of teaching," she said, sticking as close to the truth as possible. "I wanted to be a mother." When he looked up at her across the table, she nodded. "I know. No one thinks of motherhood as a career today, but I did. I suppose because I remembered my mom so clearly, and really missed the softness and the sweetness that went with her when she died. I wanted to re-create that for someone else."

AMOS HAD NO DIFFICULTY understanding that. "I remember my mother very clearly, too. I remember the way she smelled...powdery or something. She had this giant puff thing she used, and the bathroom was a cloud of powder when she was finished. She used to pat me with it when I was really small, then when I got to be seven or eight, I told her it was girl stuff and I didn't want her to do it anymore. After she died, I'd have have given anything to let her do it one more time."

"I'm sorry." Meg sipped at her wine, the candlelight doing wondrous things to her hair. "At least I still had my father. And my brothers."

Amos nodded. "I'd have given a lot for a sibling in those days. But the kids at the ranch became my family. All in all, my childhood turned out all right. I had caring support, and the staff saw that I had a lot of opportunities."

On the tip of his tongue was an admission he seldom shared with anyone, but these few days were supposed to be about sharing and honesty—and she'd paid big bucks for it.

"If anything," he said, watching her split a roll in half, "I miss family more now than I did then. When I was a boy, the staff kept us busy. Later, when I was in school, it took every waking moment just to keep up with studies and a part-time job, and when I first started the business, it consumed me."

Meg buttered her roll, then put it on the edge of her plate and gave him her full attention. He liked the way she did that, as though he actually were an authority she hoped to learn from.

"Certainly you're too successful now to be lonely," she said.

"Success in business doesn't do much for you after dinner when the house is empty, or in the middle of the night when you're alone in a bed."

She sighed. "Nothing can make loneliness feel better. I know that."

He knew she was lonely. Every once in a while he caught a glimpse of the fear in her that probably stemmed from something unfulfilled inside her. He just didn't understand why. "But you said you have your father and brothers."

She nodded quickly. "They're wonderful, but that's not the kind of loneliness I'm talking about. I mean, parents and siblings are such a blessing, but even with them, when you get right down to it, you're still isolated in this little tube of life, and when you can't find the one person who can fit in that space with you, you feel alone." She frowned as she spoke, her blue eyes troubled, then she seemed to come to, surprised that she'd revealed so much. She picked up one half of her roll and frowned at it. "I think that's why people make such terrible mistakes in relationships. Even people from stable, comfortable homes. They want that connection so badly that they reach for the first glimpse of kindness and understanding, and hold on to it, even when it becomes clear that it's not what they thought it was."

"Is that what happened to you?" he asked gently. "And this cerebral Daniel?"

"I'm not sure," she admitted, taking a bite of her roll. She chewed and thought. "He was a lawyer and represented one of my students who'd shot her husband in self-defense," she said finally. "He seemed heroic then, battling for her in the courtroom. He was very good."

"But?"

"I don't know. I didn't have any second thoughts about him. He just had them about me, apparently. It's embarrassing to find out that something so enormous was missing between us that he fell in love with someone else so quickly and so completely and I wasn't even aware of it!''

"I think it's safe to say that whatever was missing was in him. If he thought something was wrong, why didn't he tell you about it? And he had to have already been seeing the other woman for him to have left with her a week before *your* wedding day. He sure doesn't sound like a monument to good character to me. Why do you blame yourself for any of it?''

She looked him in the eye. "She's fifteen years older than I am.''

"Would you feel any better about it if she was the same age as you are?''

She smiled in self-deprecation. "I'm supposed to be in my sexual prime. But he took off with a woman who's almost middle-aged. Not that I think older women aren't sexy, but how often do men leave young women for *older* ones?''

"I guess as often as the older woman has whatever it is he's looking for. I presume this was in San Francisco?''

"Yes.''

"What's her name?''

"Cloris Biederman.''

Amos rolled his eyes, suddenly understanding the jerk who'd walked away from Meg. "Don't you know who she is?'' he asked. "The Fox Fine Foods heiress.''

She shook her head, clearly puzzled. "I don't travel in those circles. I'd never heard of her until I called his office the day we were supposed to get our license to find out where he was.''

"She and I have been to some of the same parties."
He shrugged. "She's fun, very glamorous, but very
into having what she wants. I'd say cerebral Daniel
left you for her money and social position and is probably already regretting it. She's had three husbands
that I know of, and usually a pool boy or a golf pro
on the side."

"You're kidding!"

"I'm not. She's a randy lady. And she's more like
twenty years older than you. But I don't think you
should worry about it anymore. Daniel's history.
Right now you're like one of the women you're working with—in transition from the old life to the new
one. Time to make a new set of plans, build new
dreams."

She seemed to consider that while spearing a brussels sprout. "Is that what you did when you broke up
with Jillian?"

"Uh...no. I decided to just back off for a while.
We have a new product line this year and I've been
swamped."

She studied him evenly. "What about after dinner
in an empty house and in the middle of the night?"

He couldn't tell her he'd accepted that rather than
risk being hurt and betrayed again. That wasn't exactly heroic advice for the women in her class.

"I guess I have to live with it for a while," he
said.

Her sudden smile was understanding. "Being over-
turned for design plans was no less painful than being
left for another woman, was it? Particularly when you
had no family to hold your hand."

He shook his head and told her what he always tried to remind himself. "Nobody can hurt you if you refuse to let yourself be hurt."

She laughed softly and held up her bandaged index finger. "I might have believed that if I hadn't just impaled my finger on a fishhook. Anything can hurt you, anytime. You may decide not to let it haunt you forever, but it's going to hurt."

He studied her in surprise, feeling more like her student than the man who was supposed to teach her about relationships. "That's very worldly-wise," he said.

She dismissed the praise and lifted her wineglass toward him. "To new dreams?" she suggested.

He liked that, but he refined it a little. "To intersecting dreams," he said, touching the lip of her glass with his. "Ours."

CHAPTER SIX

IT WAS AFTER ELEVEN when Meg called her father. She'd helped Amos clean up, choosing to ignore his toast about intersecting dreams. Tension was building between them already in the softly lit cabin and she had to keep her wits about her.

She tried her best to keep her emotional objectivity, but Amos was always drawing her into the warmth of his personal space and distracting her from what should be a vigilant awareness.

If she let herself succumb to it, he might be in danger. But if she resisted too hard, he might become suspicious about why she'd invited him and begin to question everything surrounding these few days.

So she had to walk a fine line. She took a step in that direction by locking up the cabin and going to bed early. Mercifully, he did the same. She waited for an hour or so until the cabin was completely quiet, then went into the living room and double-checked the windows and door. She peered outside, but saw nothing in the darkness.

Once she was back in her room, she stabbed out her father's number on her cell phone.

"Hey!" he greeted her, whispering as she did. "How's it going?"

"Very well," she replied. "What's happening with Jillian?"

"I'm not sure. She didn't follow you after the auction like I thought she might, but she's stayed home from the office for a few days, so I've been staked out in front of her house. The word at Chayco is that she has the flu."

"Hmm. Do you think it's the jealous flu and she's planning retribution because I outbid her?"

"Anything's possible, so keep your eyes open in case something gets by me."

"Right."

"And speaking of which..." His voice, still soft, took on a lighter note. "You owe me five thousand dollars."

She laughed. "Take it out of my expense account. My job was to end up with Amos Pike and I did, so I don't see how you can complain."

"How'd you get him to the cabin?"

She cleared her throat, then told him what she'd told Amos. There was a momentary silence.

"And how's that going?" He sounded worried.

"Fine," she replied. "He's very willing to help me."

"I'll bet he is."

"What does that mean?"

"Nothing. Like I said, just watch yourself."

"I'm watching, I'm watching. Don't nag."

"I'm not nagging. And I know you hate it when I say this, but if you get to feeling you might need help, just say the..."

"I do not need help!" This time her whisper was

close to a shout. "Do not send Ben and Brian, do you hear me? I'm doing fine."

"All right, all right. I just want you to know it's an option."

"I know it's an option. But if you send them, I'll shoot them."

"Meggie..."

"I've got to go, Dad. I'll call you tomorrow."

She heard her father sigh. "I love you, Meg."

"I know, Dad. I love you, too. Good night."

Meg tucked the phone away in her backpack, checked under her sweater at the bottom to make sure her Smith & Wesson 669 was accessible, pulled out a Midnight Louie mystery and began to read. She was asleep by the third page.

MEG AWOKE TO a surreptitious sound beyond her door. Her room was still dark, the frail predawn light barely a slit on the horizon. She got silently out of bed and listened, trying to locate the sound. It was difficult to be sure with the cabin's thick walls, so she turned the knob slowly and pulled the door open.

Her eyes met total darkness, but she heard a small bump from the direction of the kitchen. Either the raccoons were back, she speculated, or Amos was up early.

But if Amos was up, why hadn't he put a light on?

There was a third alternative. Jillian had somehow found out where Meg had taken him and was out for retribution after all. Or for the design.

Her father said Jillian hadn't followed her, but that didn't mean she hadn't found out about the Loria summer place and sent out the same goons she'd hired to mug Amos in the parking garage.

She moved silently toward the kitchen, noticed that the back door was open several inches and steadied herself as her heart lurched. Then she felt the slight disturbance of air behind her and to the right, a sigh of sound like something moving through that space, and flung a curled fist out to connect with something solid.

Her arm was caught and held but she thrust out a foot and delivered a kick to where she estimated the groin area to be.

A rewarding "Oof!" of pain from a male voice sounded in the darkness.

An amateur, she thought smugly, then a toe curled around her ankle and tried to bring her down.

She hurled out her other arm, but as she used his weight to give power to her thrust, her opponent lost balance and, their legs entangled, they went down together.

She landed on top and pressed her forearm against her opponent's throat, forcing her index knuckle against his temple. "Don't move a muscle," she threatened, "or I'll blow you away!" He didn't have to know he was in danger from a .22-caliber finger.

To her complete surprise, her captive didn't move except to draw a labored breath. "Good morning, Meg," he said in a strangled voice.

For an instant she couldn't move. Then she silently called herself all kinds of stupid and got up on her knees astride his waist.

"Amos?" she demanded, as angry with him as she was with herself.

There was another labored breath. "You were expecting maybe a rapist or a murderer?"

She leapt to her feet and went to the light just inside the kitchen. The glaring track lights over the counter revealed Amos supine on the floor in khaki shorts and a white T-shirt. He grimaced against the light as he got to his feet.

"What are you doing up at this hour?" she demanded. "Why didn't you put a light on? Why is the back door open? You've never heard of identifying yourself when you're attacked?"

He winced as he stood, then bent over, his hands braced against his thighs as he drew deep breaths. "It's almost five," he replied, pausing to blow out a breath. "I'm always up at this hour. I didn't...put a light on because I didn't want to disturb you." He straightened as he blew out another breath. "The back door is open because I love the smell of morning." He focused on her, his expression wry and amusedly critical. "When you're being punched in the solar plexus or kicked in your...pride, it doesn't occur to you to say, 'Hey there, I'm Amos Pike. You got anger issues you want to talk about?'"

Embarrassed and still annoyed, she glared at him. "I'm sorry. I heard noises."

He spread his arms. "It didn't occur to you that it could be me and not an intruder?"

"I...forgot you were here," she fibbed, instead of admitting that sometimes alertness could be honed to too fine a point.

He folded his arms and shook his head. "Well, that hurts my feelings. I thought about *you* all night long."

Her anger evaporated in the sudden current generated by his remark. "If you came into the kitchen and opened the back door," she said, trying to evade the pull of his watchful eyes, "why were you behind me when I walked into the kitchen?"

"That's simple." He looked around him for something on the floor, then spotted a small plump bag that must have fallen from his hands and slipped under the table in their scuffle. He retrieved it and held it up to show her. "French roast coffee. I remembered that you have that wimpy hazelnut stuff and went back to my room to get this."

She raised an eyebrow and he said in an aside, "I know, I know. But allow me my eccentricities. Traveling with my own coffee is one of them." That explanation finished, he went on. "When I came back to the kitchen, I thought I heard something, but before I could say anything, I got the heel of your hand to my clavicle." He rubbed the spot at his throat where she'd struck him. The T-shirt he wore was molded to his well-defined torso, and he didn't look as though she'd done him much harm. "I'm sorry I frightened you. Did Steven Segal teach the classes you took, or are you just a brilliant student?"

"I give everything I try my wholehearted effort," she said grimly, then added on a defensive note, "I'm sorry about the kick."

He headed toward the coffeepot. "I'll recover. But someday we'll have to apply that wholehearted effort of yours to another purpose. I'll get breakfast if you want to shower.''

Meg didn't argue but made a hasty escape.

Maybe she just wouldn't report in to her father today, she thought as she stood under the hot spray. How would she explain that she'd posed more of a threat to their client's safety than his enemies had?

What was wrong with her? She knew you never struck or used a weapon until you'd identified the target.

But it had been dark, she reminded herself. And she'd meant to protect him. Of course, he didn't know that. He probably thought she was just some paranoid freak who'd paid a bundle for him, then spirited him away for a week to torture him.

She let the water beat on her scalp in an attempt to drum away the memory of her performance and the knowledge of how amused her brothers would be if they knew.

Unable to stall any longer, she dried herself off, changed into jeans and a white shirt, wound her wet hair up in a tight knot, then strode back into the kitchen, head held high. She'd half expected to find him packing to leave, but he'd set the table with bowls and spoons, fresh fruit, cereal and milk.

"I'm sorry, Amos," she said again, sincerely this time.

He pulled out her chair in the same courtly manner he'd employed the night before. "You're forgiven. And it was my fault as much as yours. And I might say that you're pretty dexterous for a woman who carved up her finger yesterday." He sat across from her and grinned as she passed him the cereal. "So," he said. "You got anger issues you'd like to talk about?"

She laughed. "Actually, I do," she said. "After last night's dinner, I thought maybe we'd have eggs Benedict or something for breakfast. At least French toast. And let's be accurate about this. I caught my finger. *You* carved it up."

"Sorry." He passed her the milk. "How is it today?"

"A little sensitive, but healing, thank you. About this monastery breakfast…"

"I know cereal isn't very romantic, but it's intended to provide fuel for romance this morning."

She stopped with the milk jug in one hand and the cap in the other. "It is?"

He cut a banana in two and reached across the table to slice one half into her bowl in neat eighth-inch disks. "Yeah. I thought we'd take a walk this morning."

"Walking is romantic?"

"Hand in hand it is."

"Ah. Well." She poured the milk into her bowl. "Please don't feel you have to be Don Juan every moment of the day. I do want to know what men want in a woman, but I also know that relationships aren't *all* about romance."

He sliced the other half of the banana into his bowl. "You mean because of cerebral Daniel?"

"I mean because it's also about who's willing to take out the garbage or change the diapers or be the first one up on a winter morning to turn up the heat."

"Sure it is," he agreed, "but love is behind all that, and it's the romance in a lover that makes you want to manifest it. Otherwise you become one of those people who can't say 'I love you,' or never compliments a good meal or tells you you look pretty or handsome. Who wants that?"

THE SUN WAS UP, but the morning air still held a chill when they left the house. Amos's backpack held a thermos with the leftover coffee, a couple of sandwiches and two apples. In Meg's was a blanket for sitting and, in a side pocket, her telephone and her weapon.

When they walked through town, all the commercial buildings were still closed except for the supermarket. Behind the door a round, bespectacled man turned the Closed sign to Open and waved at them through the glass.

Beyond town, a boy on a bike rode by, flinging the morning paper onto porches and doorsteps. A man in a red robe came out of a white frame house with green shutters, a little black-and-white puppy on a leash.

"In San Francisco," Amos said as they headed for the trees at the edge of town, "the sidewalks would already be congested with people on their way to work. Horns would be honking, you'd hear the cable car."

Meg looked up at him, intrigued. "You sound homesick."

"No." He shook his head. "But I like the fact that the town's awake all night. You can't help but catch the excitement."

"Do you need excitement?"

"No." He laughed. "Just company, I guess."

Amos pointed off the road to their left toward a field of daisies and bluebells. Behind it was a forest of lodgepole pines. "According to my map, there's a stream off in that direction. Do you know it?"

She shook her head. "When I come here for any length of time, I spend most of it on the lake. You have a map?"

He was surprised that she was surprised. "Yes. I had originally thought I might sightsee while I was here."

"But you knew you were being auctioned off."

"Yeah, but I didn't know it would involve my being spirited off to a cabin for a week."

She smiled at him as he took her hand and headed off among the bluebells. "That's right. You were hoping for that sex slave experience, weren't you? You thought you'd just do that for a few days, then have a little time to see the sights?"

"Something like that. It's still an option for you, you know."

"Thanks, but you're too valuable as my relationship guide."

Something burst out of a clump of brush to their left and Amos pointed to it as it arced overhead.

"Sage grouse," Meg said.

"I was thinking about producing maps for children," Amos told her, following the bird's path with his gaze before moving on. "Something bright and colorful with local flowers and animals on it and places of interest to children."

"That's a wonderful idea. Sort of like a road atlas for kids?"

"Sort of. The only thing that worries me is that I can imagine some bright little kid heading off on his own because he *has* a map, where he might not do that without one. Scare his parents to death."

"But he wouldn't get lost," she pointed out.

"No, but he'd be vulnerable to other dangers."

"True. But it's still a good idea. And kids with a tendency to wander off would do it even without a map. Ben and Frank got lost once when we were vacationing on the Oregon coast. They were exploring and got stuck on a spit of land when the tide came in."

Amos frowned. "What happened?"

"Rescue involved the Coast Guard and a helicopter. They thought it was all very exciting, but my parents were apoplectic. Brian recommended leaving the boys there. He's always been trying to cut out the competition."

Amos laughed. "Sibling rivalry is something you don't have to deal with when you're alone in the world. At the ranch we felt we were all in it together and usually did our best to help one another. There were some warring factions, of course, but generally we were mutually supportive."

"My brothers were, too, in a crunch. But when things were going well and they could beat one another out of something, it was big sport."

Amos was pleased to discover that Meg was an uncomplaining hiker and good company. She trudged over rocks, uphill and down, through tall grass and over a considerable distance without whining. Jillian had never walked anywhere if she could help it, and even the more athletic women he knew got their exercise in gyms or on formal ball courts rather than by exploring their environment.

They found the stream midmorning in a stand of cottonwoods stretched out beyond the pines. It moved lazily, the water sparkling under the bright sun as it gurgled over rocks and debris from the bank.

Amos turned to offer Meg a supporting hand down a bank thick with growth, then pulled off his pack and pointed to a flat rock. He took out the thermos of coffee and gave it to her to pour while he cut an apple in half with his Swiss Army knife. Then he sliced off a wedge, avoiding the core.

"Filleted apple," she said appreciatively. "Thank you. I'll bet Adam had to deal with seeds when Eve shared hers with him."

"And a lot of other unpleasant stuff." He sat beside her on the rock. "You're a good walker."

"I spent my childhood trying to keep up with brothers who were trying to escape me. I didn't have a choice." She laughed at herself. "When I got to be a teenager, I had to learn to reduce my stride and mince a little because I could outdistance the football coach."

He cut her another wedge of apple and offered it to her off the blade of the knife. "I thought we'd evolved to the point where a buff woman was a good thing."

"You can be buff," she explained, "but you can't outperform the guys. At least in school. Are you one of those CEOs who provide a gym for their employees?''

''We don't have a gym on-site,'' he said, taking a wedge of apple and chewing. ''But we have an employee membership at a gym two blocks away. I get there less than anybody. My assistant and her son use it a lot.''

WAS THAT BORADINO? Meg wondered. She scanned the landscape while she nibbled on the apple, one ear on Amos's conversation, the other tuned to the sounds around her. She had no reason to believe they were being watched or followed, but she'd have hated for either of those possibilities to surprise her as fact.

She'd been watching on the pretext of enjoying the scenery since they left town. At first it was simply normal precaution, but now it was a way to distract herself from Amos's insidiously appealing attentions.

She'd had male protection all her life thanks to her father and brothers, but the chivalrous attentions Amos provided were something new for her.

Though he'd experienced her ability to protect herself just this morning in the kitchen, he still offered her a hand when the going was rough, put his hands to her waist and lifted her from one rock to another when she could have leapt the distance.

He was the quintessential gentleman, and it amazed her that he remained so even after she'd decked him that morning. A similar experience had completely shaken Daniel's masculinity, but Amos's hadn't suffered at all.

It didn't seem fair to lie to such a man, but

Boradino had been certain that he'd never have willingly agreed to a bodyguard. Meg had to consider that her deception was for his own good.

"What are you looking for?" Amos asked, peering through the trees as she did. "Do bears drink from this stream or something?"

She gave him a quick smile, silently reminding herself to be more subtle. "No. It's just the teacher's frame of mind. Notice everything so you can share it with your students."

Mercifully, he seemed to accept that. "Do you ever take your ladies hiking?" he asked.

"No. But that might be a good idea if we could find the time. Most of them are single mothers who work full-time. But maybe an event planned with the children could be fun." She punched Amos's arm as he dropped the apple core into a plastic bag in his pack. "That's a good idea."

"I'm full of them." He shouldered his pack, took her hand and pulled her off the rock. "Think you can leap the stream?"

"Sure."

He jumped across first, then held his arms out to balance her as she followed him. She landed smoothly but right in the circle of his arms, her hands braced on his biceps, his firmly grasping hers.

She looked into his eyes and read the kiss there even before he lowered his mouth to hers. It was a natural progression of events—companionship, a shared adventure, celebration at the discovery of their delight in each other.

Then he caught her hand again and they walked

on. Amos set a path aimed at taking them to the far side of the lake, where they would have lunch before returning home.

Walking hand in hand *was* romantic, she decided. Daniel had never done that. He'd disliked public displays of affection. Many people knew him in town, he'd claimed, and he had a professional image to maintain.

Truth be told, he hadn't even seemed to like private displays of affection.

When they stopped for lunch, Meg discovered that Amos had made thick deli sandwiches complete with pickle and sliced green pepper. She made a sound of approval as she chewed.

He poured her a cup of coffee. "You are something," he said. "Most women of my acquaintance won't eat anything but lean turkey or that phony crab stuff. What are you making for dinner?"

She winced at him over the sandwich. "Me?"

He was lying on his side on the blanket, propped up on an elbow while she sat beside him, legs curled to the side.

"You," he said. "Romance can't be too one-sided or it won't work. It has to be reciprocal."

"Oh. Sure. Well, I warned you that I'm not great in the kitchen."

"Right. That's why I bought some canned stuff."

"Then I'll fix Monday-night surprise," she said with a smile. "Do you like hot-and-spicy stuff?"

"Yeah." He looked just a little concerned. "You're not going to try to cook Szechwan or Cajun or anything?"

"And what if I did?" She condemned his skepticism with a frown. "Part of romance is to be trusting."

He nodded quickly. "It is. But part of self-preservation is to be watchful and...informed."

"But it doesn't compute to be concerned with self-preservation when you're interested in romance, does it?" she asked candidly. "I mean, love is about having faith in the loved one."

"You're absolutely right." He held out a little bag of carrot sticks toward her. "Monday-night surprise it is, and no questions asked."

"Thank you. We can pick up Pepto-Bismol on the way home, just in case."

CHAPTER SEVEN

"YOU NEVER MENTIONED what your father does,"
Amos said. He was stuffing socks, underwear and
towels into the washer and invited her to share the
load. She tossed in the socks and shirt she'd worn
that morning and a few other things. "This place is
something else for a summer home. Is he a
plumber?" he teased. "A dentist? A computer pro-
grammer?"

What her father did. Okay. She couldn't tell him
Loria Security provided bodyguards. "He...makes...
security equipment," she said, remembering the rule
about sticking as close to the truth as possible. And
that was true, if you considered Brian and Ben. They
were rather sophisticated security equipment. "My
brothers work there, too. Except for Frank, of
course."

"Right. The priest."

Meg set the water temperature and wash cycle, then
turned the dial, and water began to flow into the machine. She led the way into the kitchen, eager to distract Amos from his line of questioning.

"My grandmother Rooney is still with us—sort
of." She pointed Amos to a kitchen chair, then dug
into a bottom cupboard for Brian's stash of hot stuff.

She found a small can of jalapeños and placed it on the counter. Then she opened the freezer, hoping Ben hadn't eaten the last of the Hot Brot.

But there it was way in the back—two pounds left. She pulled out a one-pound package then went to the cooler for the bag of red potatoes. "You aren't a purist about your food, are you?" she asked, removing the snap tie from the mesh bag. "I mean, you don't mind mixing ethnicities?"

He thought that over and said cautiously, "As long as we're not talking about gefilte fish and spaghetti."

She laughed and tossed a potato at him. "We're talking about German and Mexican. A hot sausage, potato and sauerkraut casserole with jalapeño corn bread. I know it sounds weird, but Brian got me hooked on it."

He was relieved. "No, that sounds good." He held up the potato. "Do you need me to peel this?"

"No, but if you want to scrub a few, I'd appreciate that."

"You got it. You were telling me about your grandmother Rooney."

"Oh, right." She handed him the vegetable brush, then reached into a cupboard for a baking dish. "My mom's mother. After Grandpa died, she met Ruben Ross at a line-dancing class."

Amos looked up in surprise from rinsing a potato. "Ruben Ross, the developer?"

She blinked at him. "You knew him?"

"No, just of him. He was worth a bundle."

She nodded and tried to open a jar of sauerkraut, favoring her probably still-sensitive finger. Amos was sure she could have done it eventually, but he took it from her and opened it with one sharp twist.

"Thank you," she said. "Well, now Grandma's worth a bundle. She's a major philanthropist, you know. She's traveling around right now buying art for a little museum in Shasta, California. She was going to contribute to Becky's program by funding the building of a center for women in transition. A place where women could stay until they get on their feet."

"*Was* going to fund it?"

She poured the sauerkraut into a colander, bumping his elbow as they worked together over the sink. A sensation of blissful domesticity ran along her spine.

"Well...Grandma Rooney's a dear old lady, but she's a little dotty. The funding was tied to my marriage to Daniel."

"What?"

"I know, but she's still living in her girlhood in the twenties and thirties and thinks women can't be happy or fulfilled unless they're married and raising children." She explained the binding condition on which her grandmother had made the deal. "She said if I backed out of the marriage, the center wouldn't get the money."

"And she doesn't understand that Daniel backed out on you?"

"I don't know. She's in Senegal somewhere and I haven't been able to reach her. She'll probably construe it as my fault. She's wonderful, but there's a little dementia going on there. She's generally sharp and very healthy, but she makes some weird connections sometimes, as though messages are short-circuited or something. But I'm going to try to plead my case when she comes home."

"Is she safe to travel if she's like that?"

"She has a companion, an old friend in her sixties who goes everywhere with her and tries to keep her safe."

"It sounds like a full-time job."

"I wouldn't want to have to do it."

THEY ATE AT SUNSET while sitting in the glider on the porch. Though they'd talked all afternoon, they found still more to talk about as they consumed half the casserole and a good portion of the corn bread. Amos didn't think he'd ever enjoyed a meal quite as much—and for someone who regularly enjoyed San Francisco's finest restaurants, that was saying something.

He was developing a serious affinity for this lake, this town, this cabin—and he knew it was all because he was in the company of this woman.

He wasn't sure he had the full story on why he was here, but it was beginning to matter less and less. His life had distilled to these few early summer days in the company of this beautiful redhead with all those curious things in her eyes he couldn't quite read.

It used to be so important to him to understand things, but since he'd met Meg Loria, he seemed to have turned a page in his development. He could accept things and people he didn't understand. He could befriend them. He was even beginning to think he could love them and contemplate a lifetime with them.

It seemed wise, however, to keep that to himself for now. She enjoyed being kissed by him, and she made subtle emotional advances toward him, but they were usually followed by retreats. And that was something he thought he should understand before he told her that he was taking her home with him when he left.

After dinner they walked to the ice cream counter in the supermarket and carried back ice cream cones. Hers was straight vanilla, his vanilla and chocolate.

"I love chocolate, too," she said as they wandered down the walk toward the pier. "But nothing's quite as decadent as good vanilla."

"Decadence is important to you?" he teased.

She nodded seriously. "It's one of those things you can't do halfway. You can be moderately bad, but you can't be decadent unless you go over the edge." She smiled at him as they walked to the edge of the pier. "See? I have a few things to teach you, too."

The sun had set and dusk advanced in an irregular mass of dark blue that came up from behind the mountains and inched its way toward them. They sat side by side on the edge of the wooden planks, feet dangling just above the water.

A small boat headed across the lake, running lights bright in the encroaching darkness. He felt Meg sit up straighter and tense just a little as it went past.

"Someone you know?" he asked.

It seemed to take her a moment to register the question, her attention completely absorbed by the small, slow-moving craft.

"No," she replied finally. "I...was just wondering

if we were about to have company.'' She smiled suddenly, bumping him with her shoulder. ''What do you want to do tomorrow?''

''We did what I wanted to do today. We should do what you want to do tomorrow.''

''Shampoo our hair and watch soaps?''

He laughed. ''Okay, maybe we could reach some kind of compromise.''

''Good.'' Her ice cream finished, she angled her left leg on her right knee and pulled off her tennis shoe and sock. ''I think I'm getting a blister on this foot.''

He leaned over her to try to see in the dim light. ''That's because you should hike in boots and not tennis shoes.''

''Well, I didn't know that walking hand in hand and talking about relationships was going to involve five miles over hill and dale. Usually romantic walks end up on a park bench or in a little sidewalk café. Ouch.'' She winced as he rubbed his thumb over the blister.

''Sorry. I did bring you to the edge of a pier at sunset.'' He indicated the now-darkening sky and the lights of the cabins visible on the opposite bank. ''And I had every intention of taking advantage of the moment until you brought up the blister.''

CONVINCED THE LITTLE BOAT did *not* pose a threat of any kind, Meg was just beginning to relax again. But Amos was very close to her suddenly, a hand still holding her ankle, and everything inside her began to riot.

"You were?" she breathed.

"I was," he replied quietly, his hand moving from her ankle to cup her cheek.

"Well...go a—"

"Shh."

It was a sultry, summer-night kiss, she thought, as the tenderness of it threatened to rob her of her awareness. She felt herself drawn into his touch, just as his eyes always seemed to pull her into him. He had a knack of making her forget herself and presenting the enticing possibilities of what he and she could be together.

For a moment, she let those possibilities take control. As his hands moved gently but possessively over her, she leaned into him, letting it happen, drawn by the eagerness to know where it would lead.

She could feel every one of his fingertips against her back and her cheek, smell the pine and wildflower sweetness of the night air, hear the gentle lap of water against the pier and feel the beginning of her own surrender.

He'd kissed her before, but this was something else. It wasn't exploration as much as communication, a mutual meeting of emotion and need that seemed to be fusing them together in a new and urgent way that would never result from conversation and camaraderie.

With sudden awareness, she realized the danger this presented to his safety and—on another level entirely—her own. Resolutely, she wedged a space between them. He looked into her eyes, still holding her loosely in his arms.

It was impossible for her to read his face in the darkness. But she could sense his annoyance at her withdrawal from what had felt like a significant moment for them.

"Come on." He got to his feet and helped her up. "Let's go back. There must be something in that medicine cabinet for your blister."

"Wait," she began, reaching down in the almost total darkness. "My shoe and my... Oops." There was the sound of a very small "plop."

"What?" he asked, his tone mildly impatient.

"Lost my sock over the side," she said with a small laugh.

For the second time in as many days, he swung her up into his arms and carried her toward the cabin.

"I'm beginning to feel like Viking plunder or something," she joked, holding on, wanting to lighten the moment.

"Tomorrow," he answered, striding easily toward the cabin's back door, "I'm going to see if I can sell you off across the lake."

"Wouldn't you rather keep me as a slave?"

"How would we explain that to your students?"

"True."

He sat her on the closed lid of the john while he rummaged in the medicine cabinet. The brightly lit bathroom in cheerful pastels and whimsical underwater wallpaper seemed alien with him in it.

At the moment her entire life was alien. She was sitting in the bathroom with the gorgeous CEO of a toy company, a shoe in her hand, her heart in her mouth.

He sat opposite her on the rim of the tub, washed her blistered heel with a warm cloth, dried it, then applied an antibiotic cream and a bandage.

"All right," he said, getting to his feet and tossing the wrapper in the wastebasket. "That should do it." He replaced the cream in the cabinet. His manner and his movements were stiff.

"Thanks," she said. She could have easily looked after her foot herself, but she was touched that, even angry with her, he'd provided that small service. "I'll have to tell my ladies to watch for a man with medical skills."

About to walk out of the bathroom, he stopped suddenly in the doorway and turned to face her, blocking her exit.

"You aren't mistaking me for one of them, are you?" he asked, frowning.

She blinked in confusion. "One of whom?"

"The losers your women in transition have hooked up with who've ruined their lives." He folded his arms and leaned a shoulder against the doorjamb, apparently determined to have this out in the most unlikely of places.

Meg braced herself, trying not to panic. She couldn't explain to him why she'd withdrawn from that promising kiss, so she would have to keep her wits about her.

"I know that happens," he continued. "Women see other women go through all kinds of hell because of a man who treats them badly or walks away, and they begin to think all men are like that. It's probably a particular problem in your work, where that's *all* you see. And Daniel confirmed that for you.''

''I don't have you confused with Daniel,'' she assured him firmly, ''or any other man in the world, for that matter. You're too unique for that.''

That seemed to soften his features slightly, though she wasn't sure it diminished his annoyance with her.

''Then what kind of a game are we playing here?'' he asked, his gaze steady.

''I explained...'' she began, but he cut her off abruptly.

''I know, and that may or may not be true. I haven't decided. But there's something going on here on a personal level that you seem to be trying to manipulate.''

That made her blink again. ''What do you mean?''

''Are you a virgin?'' he asked without preamble.

''What!'' She was surprised by the indignation she felt. She had *some* experience. Not much, but some. And there was something embarrassing about being mistaken for a woman who had none. It was also her biggest fear—that her motherless childhood and her overprotective father and brothers had made her somehow asexual.

''Why?'' she demanded. ''Because I bought you at an auction? I think it's dirty old men who pay a high price for virgins!''

He was unimpressed by her anger. ''Not because of the auction,'' he replied calmly, ''but because you keep moving toward me, coming closer, and every time I respond, you back off. It's as though you're setting up a scene, then you lose your nerve when I take my role. Did you pay ten thousand dollars for a man who makes games for a living, presuming that he would therefore be willing to play them?''

She struggled to hold her temper, knowing she couldn't be angry at him for jumping to faulty conclusions when he wasn't aware of all the facts.

"I paid ten thousand dollars for you," she said, "because according to the claims of all your admirers, you're a nice man. That's what I wanted to learn about. It had nothing to do with me personally."

She thought she'd stated that very convincingly, but he stared her down until she was forced to shift her weight, look away, then look back at him again and admit a little defensively, "Okay, in the beginning it wasn't personal. But now it's...getting to be."

He drew a breath, apparently somewhat appeased by that admission. "All right. Now we're getting somewhere. So, why did that kiss scare you?"

"Because...vulnerability is scary. Isn't it scary to you?"

He narrowed his eyes, apparently giving that serious thought. "It shouldn't be. At this stage of a relationship, trust should make vulnerability acceptable. But you clearly don't trust me. One minute you look at me as though I'm the most important discovery you've ever made, and the next you stiffen up and seem scared to death of me." His mouth twisted wryly. "You can understand why that confuses me and makes me wonder if it's safe to trust you."

She didn't know what to say to that without having to admit too much. She finally settled for, "I would never hurt you, Amos."

He didn't seem convinced of that. "You mean you would never intend to. I've been tricked before, remember?"

She decided instantly that he had taught her something about trust, so she took a chance that even if she gave him a way out, he wouldn't take it. "And I've been walked out on before. If you think you're being used for some unsavory purpose—" she pointed toward the living room and the front door "—you're free to go."

She felt the seconds tick away as they stared into each other's eyes, and she wondered in a panic if she should be preparing to explain to her father how she'd lost their client and put his life at risk.

Then, to her complete surprise, Amos smiled. "Unsavory?" He repeated her word with amusement. "I would never consider your wanting me to introduce you to lovemaking as unsavory."

Indignation flared up in her again. She let it have its head so that he wouldn't see her relief that he hadn't grabbed the opportunity and walked out the door. She put both hands to his chest and pushed him out of her way. "I do not have to be *introduced* to lovemaking, thank you very much. I am not a virgin." She marched down the hallway to the dark living room and walked around, flipping on lights.

"Really." He followed her and stood in the middle of the room, watching her. "How many times?"

She stopped and turned to him in disbelief at that question.

"Well," he said with a grin, "you said you've been introduced. So you've done it once?"

She gasped. "Do I really seem that inexperienced to you?"

"Guileless," he corrected her. "And only when you're in my arms. Besides, you're the one who told me Daniel was cerebral."

Meg was horrified to feel herself blush to the roots of her hair. She marched off to the kitchen and went to the sink to fill the kettle.

Amos followed and leaned against the counter beside her as she put the kettle on a burner and turned it on. He caught her chin between his thumb and forefinger and looked down into her still-hot blush.

"He *didn't* make love to you?" he asked.

She pulled his hand away and walked around him to get cups. "Yes, he did. He just didn't seem to have much enthusiasm for it."

There was silence for a moment, then Amos said with flattering disbelief, "You're kidding."

She put two cups on the counter and took down a box of orange spice tea. "I'm not. I got home the day he left me at the courthouse and found a fax from him that said he'd decided after all that I didn't have a romantic bone in my body. That I could..." She stopped herself before quoting that she could outshoot him, afraid it would give something away. But Amos knew about her martial arts skills. "I could throw him or pin him every time, and Cloris never thought of doing that."

"Come on, Meg," he scolded gently as he watched her put the bags in the cups. "You know that there's something wrong with a man who feels diminished by a woman's skills. If that carried over into the bedroom and he blamed you for it, that was his problem and not yours.''

She stopped fidgeting with the cups and expelled a breath, looking up at him reluctantly. ''I know that in my heart, it's just that...I missed my mom when I was growing up, and I was surrounded by men who are dear and sweet, but all guy, and I feel...sort of...''

She had his complete attention while she groped for the words to describe how she felt. A corner of her mind not occupied with her own mortification realized that it wasn't safe for her to be this distracted. But he always did this to her—made her look inward at herself.

He didn't prod her, he simply waited.

''Sexless, I guess,'' she finally admitted in an agitated rush. ''And yes, I guess I was taking advantage of your being here to...experiment a little. To see if...you reacted to me. But not just because you're a man,'' she added quickly, candidly, ''but because you're you. And then you did, and I did, and...'' She was making no sense; she knew that. And he was watching her as though desperately trying to understand what she was saying. ''But I withdrew from that kiss,'' she continued, only half-honestly, ''because I could see where it could lead and that didn't seem fair to you.''

He frowned at that. ''Because you don't really feel anything?''

''No,'' she said. ''Because I do. But I'm too confused about what I'm doing and you're probably right not to trust me.''

He smiled again. She was beginning to notice that

his smile always made her feel as though the sun had come up. "I usually decide what's fair to me. And I do trust you, if you'll continue to be honest with me."

Honest, she thought guiltily. She wondered if he'd eventually understand that she'd lied to him for his own safety. Considering he hadn't wanted a bodyguard in the first place, she rather doubted it.

"Thanks," she said, then turned to the whining kettle, hoping that would put an end to this confusing and unsettling conversation.

She was surprised when it did. She spread out the evening paper on the kitchen table, and he took out a book he'd brought and settled in a corner of the sofa.

She went to bed just before ten and stared into the darkness until she was sure Amos had gone to bed. Then she called her father. The connection was noisy.

"Where are you?" she asked.

"At Ms. Boradino's," he said. "How's it going?"

"All right. Who's watching Jillian?"

"Ben."

Great, she thought. The world's biggest playboy staking out San Francisco's most clever seductress. They were all in trouble.

"Anything wrong?" her father asked after a moment.

"No," she replied. "It's been perfectly peaceful."

"So you're having a good time?"

She wouldn't say that. "I got a fishhook in my finger and a blister from hiking."

"Are you all right?"

"He took the hook out."

"Pike?"

"Yes. You heard anything from Grandma?"

"Uh, no. Meg, are you sure you're all right?"

Suddenly the hackneyed question had serious significance. Was she all right? Would she ever be all right again after spending time with Amos Pike and seeing what life with such a man could be like?

"I'm fine," she said, chiding herself for forgetting that at the bottom of the churning confusion of the last few days, Amos Pike was a job, and nothing else meant anything until she had safely and successfully completed it. "I've got to go."

"Meggie…"

"Bye, Dad."

She hung up, tucked the phone into the backpack by her bed, checked for the weapon at the bottom of her bag, then turned out the light.

CHAPTER EIGHT

AMOS AWOKE TO THE SOUND of rain beating against the roof and the windows. He got up in surprise and drew the curtains back. Rain struck the glass, leaving dots and dashes, and beyond it an angry gray sky had turned the sunny lakeside into a gloomy landscape.

He was surprised to see that his bedside clock read seven-thirty. He never slept this late, but then at home he didn't usually lie awake at night thinking about a beautiful redhead who blushed when she talked about lovemaking.

Anger boiled in him when he thought about the man who'd left her at the courthouse, then *faxed* her to make it clear it had all been her fault.

He was going to have to convince her that it wasn't. He was just waiting for the right moment.

He pulled on jeans and a sweatshirt and went out into the kitchen, expecting to see Meg sitting at the table over a bowl of cereal. Her room had been so quiet he'd been sure she was up.

But the kitchen was empty. Only the sound of drumming rain filled the quiet room.

As he walked back into the living room, he noticed the damp chill. Even though it was June, a fire would warm the cabin and the atmosphere.

The seasoned wood in the log carrier caught quickly, and he had a cheerful blaze going in a matter of minutes. They could eat on a blanket in front of it. Then he might be able to get this day going in a direction that would be conducive to teaching Meg she wasn't sexless at all, but a warm and responsive woman.

And a late-sleeping one this morning, he thought, when there was still no sound from her room.

He went to knock on her door to ask her what she wanted for breakfast. When there was no response, he turned the knob, found the door unlocked and peered inside.

The room was empty, the covers thrown back, Meg's pajamas in a heap in the middle of the bed as though she'd changed and left in a hurry. Her bathroom was empty.

Beginning to worry, he even checked the extra bedrooms. They were both empty. Meg was not in the house.

Walking more quickly, he went to the living room window and looked out at the driveway. The Jeep was still there, so she hadn't left in the car. But where was she?

He went back to his room for a jacket, then walked out the front door to check the pier. It was empty, and the little boat was still tied to it.

What in the hell…?

Now running, he went to the road, looked up and down it and didn't see a soul. He went around to the back of the house and stopped to listen, but all he could hear was the drumming of the rain.

In unguarded moments, he remembered, Meg would often stand by the kitchen window and look out at the woods. Had she headed off for a walk before it started raining? That seemed like a possibility until he remembered the blister on her heel.

Maybe she'd gone to town to the market? But on foot in the rain? He was about to head off in that direction when he heard a crashing in the woods. He turned back, his heartbeat accelerating, and ran toward the sound.

"Meg?" he shouted. "Meg!"

She emerged from the woods just as he reached it. Her shirt and jeans were drenched and clinging. She was limping, and her left side was splattered with mud as though she had fallen and skidded. Her hair hung around her face and shoulders in sodden, dripping strips.

"What are you doing?" he demanded, taking her arm and pulling her back toward the house even as he questioned her.

She gave him an impatient look as he ripped off his jacket and held it over her. "Could we talk about it inside? Don't do that. I'll only get your jacket all…"

He ignored her, relieved beyond describing to see her safe and sound, though her wet and muddy condition posed other questions he wanted answered. He drew her through the kitchen to the fireplace and stopped her there while he went to get a towel. As an afterthought, he ripped the blanket off his bed and carried that, too, into the living room.

She was shivering, a hand braced against the stones

of the fireplace as she pulled off her second shoe and tossed it next to the other on the hearth. She hadn't bothered with socks when she'd dressed, and she'd lost the bandage on her heel. The blister was a livid red.

"I thought you were shampooing your hair and watching soaps today," he said, tossing the blanket at a chair and draping the towel over his shoulder. "Get out of those wet things."

She looked up at him, water beading on her face and making spikes of her eyelashes. Her eyes held a curious combination of anger and fear as she resisted his efforts to unbutton her shirt.

But she'd frightened him and he was impatient with her modesty. "What were you doing in the rain?" he asked again, brushing her hands away as she tried to interfere with his. "Will you stop it? You're going to catch pneu—"

He stopped abruptly when his hands, dodging hers at the top button of her blouse, reached to the bottom button instead and encountered something metallic and hard tucked into the waistband of her jeans.

He held the wet fabric aside and found himself staring at the handle of a Smith & Wesson pocket automatic.

For a minute he couldn't process the sight— couldn't imagine what it meant. It even distracted him from the sight of her small, round breasts rising from beige lace cups.

The beautiful redhead with fear in her eyes was armed?

MEG FORCED HER BRAIN into action. It didn't want to work. She was tired and cold and very worried about the surreptitious movement she thought she'd seen on the edge of the woods when she got up to make coffee.

She'd run out to check—an action she was sure her father wouldn't approve of. She should have sat tight and waited, let them come to her. But she'd found nothing, and now she didn't know if she'd imagined the whole thing, or if she'd scared off whoever was out there.

The most important thing at the moment was that Amos not suspect who she was. If he took off in anger and there was someone out there, he'd be in danger.

He took the gun carefully from her belt and placed it on the mantel. Then he helped her get her blouse off and wrapped her in the blanket. "I thought you weren't playing games," he said coolly.

"I'm not." She felt testy, but he held the blanket closed in front of her so she could wriggle out of her jeans. It was hard to be angry at him when he did that.

"Then what in the hell are you doing running around at seven-thirty in the morning, in the woods, in the *rain*, with a gun?"

She told herself she could do this. She'd performed her way out of several scrapes as a child and a teenager with a look of innocence and a quiet explanation that caught her father and her brothers off guard.

She gave Amos a quick glance, then lowered her eyes again, knowing that eyelashes could be just as effective when the moment was right. "I thought I

saw a puppy,'' she began, the jeans wriggled down
to her knees.

Amos didn't swallow it. "So you chased it with a
gun?"

She gave him another blast of her blue eyes, this
one not quite as carefully calculated, then reached one
hand out of the blanket to steady herself on his arm
while she stepped out of her jeans.

"No," she said patiently. "The raccoons chased it
and I didn't want them to make a meal of him. So I
went after them."

"You chased raccoons into the woods with a revolver to protect a puppy." He made it sound as
though she'd reported abduction by aliens.

"Yes."

"Where's the puppy?"

"I didn't find him."

"I can't believe a puppy would have run from
you."

"If he was being chased by raccoons, he would
have."

"I didn't hear any gunshots."

She condemned his skepticism with another look.
"I told you. I didn't find them." She kicked the wet
jeans aside and drew the blanket more tightly around
her.

"Meg," he said, hands on his hips. "That is the
most pathetic..."

"It's the truth!" she lied in a loud voice, desperate
to convince him. "The woods are full of wildlife,
some friendly, some not! There's a big raccoon pop-

ulation here and the older males will fight anything for food. I'm telling you, the puppy was in trouble!''

He still didn't look convinced and tried to undermine her from another angle. "Why do you even have a gun?''

That was easy to lie around. "My father has always kept one here and taught us all to use it.''

"Even the priest?''

"If you don't believe me,'' she shouted at him, "why don't you just come out and say so?''

"I don't believe you,'' he confirmed without letting a second pass. "I want to know what's going on here, Meg.''

She rolled her eyes heavenward. "Are you this suspicious with everyone?'' she demanded, then a ploy occurred to her that involved another performance. "Oh, I get it.'' She feigned hurt feelings and wounded pride with a tilt of her chin and a quiver of her lips. "You think Jillian sent me. You said so before. You think this was all an act to get you here so I could murder you in your bed for your plans to the space station. Well, if that was my mission, why are you still alive, and why was I out in the woods?''

He frowned deeply, as though trying to come up with an answer to that question. "I don't know,'' he said at last.

"Well, when you can answer that—'' she looked away from him imperiously "—you can apologize to me for calling me a liar.''

He caught the hassock with his foot and placed it in front of her. "Sit down and dry your hair,'' he said, his tone still unconvinced, still unrepentant. "I'll put on the kettle.'' He took the towel from his shoulder, dropped it onto her head and disappeared into the kitchen.

Meg went into her bedroom and locked the door, then sank onto her bed and called her father to see if he had anything to report on Jillian that might tell her whether or not she'd seen things this morning.

But he didn't answer.

AMOS TOOK DOWN TWO CUPS and the now familiar box of orange spice tea. No matter how he tried to look at it, he couldn't believe the puppy story. There were too many holes.

And he didn't think she'd been planted by Jillian, either. Considering how Jillian had used intimacy as a ploy, she had to know that would never have worked a second time. Not that he and Meg were anywhere close to being intimate.

No. It all had something to do with why he was here, why she'd paid ten thousand dollars for him at the auction, but he just couldn't put his finger on it.

The sound of the doorbell drew him out of his speculation.

He turned off the kettle, which was just about to boil, and headed for the front door. He was halfway there when Meg came out of the hallway dressed in black sweats, a brush in her hand.

"I'll get it," she said, her glance at him hostile.

For a moment his entire attention was focused on the fiery cloud of her hair. Then he saw that there was something different about her besides the fact that her hair was free.

She looked resolved, curiously energized. She tossed the brush at a chair and shooed him toward the kitchen. "I thought you were making tea," she said, going to the door.

She seemed to be waiting for him to leave before she opened it, her stance oddly protective, and a preposterous explanation for the last few days occurred to him. He instantly dismissed it, then reconsidered it when she said impatiently, "Well?"

He folded his arms and held his ground. "I'd like to see who it is," he said, taking a certain pleasure in being deliberately obstructive.

"I'd like a cup of tea," she insisted.

The doorbell rang again.

She went to the edge of the window to peer cautiously through the curtains. After uttering a word he was surprised to learn she knew, she yanked the door open.

Three men stood in the doorway. The middle one carried a soft-sided bag and offered a smile. Flanking him were two others, one with a backpack over his shoulder, the other with a duffel. Behind them, the rain had quieted to a drizzle.

"What?" she demanded irascibly.

"Hey, Meg," the more seasoned-looking of the three said as he pushed her gently aside and walked into the living room. He spotted Amos, made a point of looking apologetically surprised, and offered his hand. "Hi," he said. "I hope we're not breaking up anything. I'm Brian Loria, Meg's brother."

Amos let him play his role. This week did seem to

be about role-playing. "Amos Pike," he said, shaking hands.

"We didn't mean to intrude upon a romantic tryst," Brian continued, "but my brothers and I all managed to get a few days off together and came up to go fishing." He pointed to his companions. "Father Frank," he said of the smiling one. "And Ben."

They all shook Amos's hand, each one pretending embarrassment at the intrusion.

The family resemblance was very apparent in the color of their eyes and the varying shades of red hair. And each man, the priest included, could have been a tackle for the Chicago Bears. They were tall and muscular and moved with the ease of men accustomed to using their size.

So the preposterous answer to the questions of the last few days was correct. Meg had said her father manufactured security equipment. These were three of the finest specimens he'd ever encountered.

Amos folded his arms. "I told my staff I didn't want bodyguards," he said to Brian.

Everyone in the room froze, including Meg. Brian turned to her. "I thought he didn't know."

Meg pushed the door closed, firming her jaw at the condemning look he sent her. Then she turned her own glare on her brothers. "So did I. Of course, the sudden appearance of the three of you looking like Schwarzenegger and company wouldn't have anything to do with revealing the plan, would it? What are you doing here?"

"Dad sent us," Ben replied.

Brian and Frank turned to him in disgust.

"What?" he demanded. "He did."

Brian shook his head. "Right. And Meg really wanted to hear that. Now whatever chance we had of taking over peacefully from her is shot to hell. Good going, Ben."

Meg got toe to toe with Brian, though he stood half a head taller than she did. "You are *not* taking over from me. I was put in charge of this assignment, and I'm going to see it through!"

Brian sighed as though he'd been in this position before and didn't relish it. He glanced apologetically at Amos, then returned his attention to his sister. "Do you really think it's cool to have this argument in front of our client?"

"Would you excuse us?" Meg asked Amos.

"No," he replied. "I'd say since this concerns me and everyone's thwarted *my* wishes in the matter, I'll just listen in."

Meg groaned and turned back to Brian. "You still want to take charge of his safety?"

Brian looked heavenward in supplication, then held up his backpack. "Can we at least put our things away, make a pot of coffee and talk about what to do like civilized people?"

"Civilized people," Meg said, arms folded, "don't treat their women like brainless nonentities incapable of carrying out simple tasks."

"Facing down armed goons," the priest said reasonably, "is not a simple task."

Meg turned a withering look on him. "It particularly isn't one for a priest. What are you doing here, anyway, Frank? I told you the wedding was off."

"I'd already scheduled the vacation time," he replied, "and simpleton that I am, I chose to spend that
time in the bosom of my family, band of warring
hyenas that you are. It's nice to see you, too, Meggie."

"And you." She glowered at Ben. "I thought you
and Blitzen were going to Acapulco this weekend."

"Her name's Bambi," he replied, "and I canceled
to come to your rescue. You're welcome, by the
way."

"I do not need to be rescued!" she said hotly, fo-
cusing on one brother after the other. "My God, how
old do I have to be before you trust me on a job
alone? Who saved Princess Daria when the rebels
chased her into Bloomingdale's?"

Brian made a scornful sound. "You ran into the
lingerie department dressing rooms. Even a guerrilla
soldier is reluctant to do that. Look..." He turned
from her to Amos. "Jillian Chambers has hired a jet."

Meg frowned. "To come here?"

"Presumably. She's been investigating us while
we've been watching her. I'm sure she knows who
you are now."

Meg turned to Amos, apparently just remembering
that he now knew she'd lied to him big-time. She
looked guilty and unhappy and very defensive. "I'm
sorry," she said. "Your unreasonable refusal to even
consider a bodyguard forced your staff to operate behind your back, and since they hired us, we had no
choice but to comply with their wishes."

All he could think about now was the wonderful
few days they'd spent together—and the fact that it

seemed as though it had all been a ploy to detain him. Temper ignited inside him, directed at himself as much as at her. He'd known she was hiding something, and it irritated the hell out of him that he'd refused to follow his intuition and find out the truth.

His staff had been on him about protection for a couple of weeks. Jeannette had nagged persistently. It amazed him that when she finally let up, he'd thought it was because she'd decided to respect his wishes, rather than because she'd made alternative plans.

How stupid *was* he? he wondered. Stupid enough, apparently, to have let himself—or at least his good sense—be sufficiently seduced by a beautiful woman that he forgot every self-protective instinct he'd ever had.

"So, is it Loria Security's customary operating procedure," he asked mildly, "to allow whoever's threatening your client to find out who's guarding him before the client does?"

Brian took a step forward, apparently prepared to answer the question, but Meg put a hand to the middle of his chest to stop him. "Why don't you guys put your stuff away," she said, her voice stiff and quiet, "and let me talk to Amos?"

"All right," Brian replied, "but according to their flight plan, they could be here in an hour. We have to be ready."

"How did you get here so quickly?" Meg asked, as though the question had just occurred to her.

Ben and Brian exchanged a reluctant look.

"We were waiting in Casper," Brian said. "You were never supposed to handle this alone."

Everyone waited for Meg to explode, but she said nothing. She simply drew a deep sigh, caught Amos's arm and pulled him with her into the kitchen.

IT AMAZED MEG that the kettle was still hot. She remembered that after Amos had challenged her explanation about the gun, he'd gone off to make tea. She found it unsettling that both her personal life and a part of her professional life had fallen apart in less time than it took boiling water to cool.

She made two cups of tea and carried them to the table. Amos stood at the window, his back to her.

"Please come and sit down," she said, trying to inject her voice with firmness. Her brothers had successfully undermined whatever authority she had, but she tried to exercise it, anyway. "You shouldn't be standing there. You present too clean a target."

He looked at her over his shoulder, his expression condemning. "It's a little late to worry about that," he said. "I've already taken a hit."

"Oh, stop being a baby," she chided, impatient with him for becoming an emotional problem for her now that the physical threat was immediate. And she was generally angry at everyone and everything. "If you'd had the good sense to hire someone to look out for you, this wouldn't have happened."

He turned slowly from the window, but made no move to join her. She knew it was deliberately to annoy her. He braced his hands behind him on the edge of the counter. "I'm not sure about that. My staff apparently hired you to protect me, and what have you done? The only difference between your kisses and Jillian's is that she wanted design plans and you wanted Loria Security's fee.''

Meg felt as though she were the one wearing the target. She could almost see her dream that she and this man might somehow emerge from this situation to spend their lives together dissolve into thin air.

"I did what I had to do to keep you here," she said. "And if you don't move away from the window, I'll move you myself." She made the threat with all the sincerity she could muster. She really wanted to fight someone right now.

He raised an eyebrow and held his arms out at his sides. "Oh, please," he said, quiet anger in the supplication. "Come and try it. I'd like nothing better right now than to drop you on your backside."

She sipped her tea. "You seem to be forgetting the other morning. And that was even in the dark."

"I was unprepared then. I thought you were what you seemed to be. Now I know better."

Suddenly weary of the word games, she put her cup down. "You don't know me at all," she said.

He agreed with a quick nod. "And whose fault is that?"

She slapped both hands on the table and stood. "Does that matter right now?" she demanded. "Your life is in danger! Would you get away from the damned window?"

He held his arms out again in a silent invitation for her to make him move. Physically, she knew she could have done it. Emotionally, she didn't think it was safe to touch him, because once she felt the muscled warmth right under his skin, her needy body would react to him.

She made her way to the bedrooms instead and stormed through Brian's half-opened door. He was on his cell phone. She snatched it from him, certain he was reporting to their father.

"I quit, do you hear me, Dad?" she ranted. "I will see this job through because *I* started it, but I am never—*ever*—working for you again. You never intended to use me as a bodyguard in this case, you used me as a call girl! You needed a woman to get Amos away for the weekend, but when that was accomplished and things got dangerous, you sent in the boys, because despite all the expensive training you got me, and my natural skill, you have no faith in me whatsoever. Well, if that's how you're going to treat me, I've just lost faith in you as a parent!"

There was a moment's silence on the other end of the line, then a cheerful feminine voice said, "Uh…hi, Meg."

Meg closed her eyes. The voice on the other end belonged to Jamie, Brian's wife. She sent Brian a lethal look and he shrugged, absolving himself of responsibility for her mistake.

"Hi, Jamie," she replied. "You married a Cro-Magnon misogynist, did you know that?"

"Yeah," Jamie replied with a light laugh. "I just wanted regular sex and to be able to live in San Francisco." Another brief pause. "Are you okay?"

"I'm fine. Here's Brian." Meg handed the phone back, then stormed down the hall to the fourth bedroom, which Frank and Ben were sharing. She zeroed in on Frank, who was sprawled out on one of the twin beds, his arms folded behind his head.

"I can't believe *you* would allow this to happen without expressing disapproval," she said, slapping his feet aside so she could sit on the foot of the bed. "It's morally wrong for an entire family to dismiss the value of one of its own simply because of her gender!"

Frank rolled his eyes in a very unclerical expression of impatience. "Give it up, Meggie," he said lazily. "You know we're not dismissing your value. You're the youngest and a girl, and we'll always run to your rescue, whether you need it or not."

"I don't think you're as upset about the fact that we're here to help," Ben said, pulling a gray sweater on over a T-shirt, "as you are that we interrupted your time alone with this guy. Something going on? He didn't look very happy with you when you took him into the kitchen—as though he felt...betrayed. What were you using to keep him here?"

"My *brain*, Ben!" she said, leaning toward him emphatically. "Explain to him what that is, Frank. He—"

"Guys..." a voice interrupted from the doorway.

"Oh, don't give me that," Ben retorted. "You're afraid of having a romantic relationship, so you consider it noble that you never..."

"Guys..." That voice again, but Meg was too incensed to hear it.

"What is *wrong* with you?" she shouted at Ben. "I was engaged!"

"Oh, yeah," Ben said. "Daniel Emery. What a big

emotional gamble that was. He treated you like a second cousin.''

"Ben, that's enough," Frank said mildly.

"Guys!"

This time everyone turned in the direction of the
door. Brian stood there, a hand braced against the
molding. "Where's our client?" he asked Meg.

She got to her feet, a tickle of icy fear edging along
her spine. "In the kitchen. I left him in the kitchen."

"Well, he isn't there now," Brian said. "And your
Jeep is gone, too. Now, before Dad finds out about
our Keystone Kops version of a security operation, I
think we'd better..."

Meg, Frank and Ben ran past him before he could
finish.

CHAPTER NINE

AMOS HAD NO INTENTION of leaving Bluebell Lake. He walked up and down the aisle of the supermarket, basket in hand, putting together the makings of dinner for five. But he was taking a certain satisfaction in having evaded Meg and her brothers and the imprisonment they intended for him.

If Jillian had come to Bluebell, or sent her emissaries here, he hoped they were watching him. He hoped they'd followed him here so that he could confront them once and for all—in the daylight—and have done with it.

He had more faith in his self-defense skills than his employees had. He didn't have the martial arts training Meg had, but given half a chance, he was as tough and determined as the next guy. He'd had to prove that often enough as a child.

The staff at the ranch hadn't condoned fighting and always punished those who settled disagreements that way, but in the ever-challenged hierarchy of growing boys, fistfights happened, anyway. Amos had always won, not because he was bigger or stronger, but because he'd been a combative little cuss with a lot to prove.

Competing as an adult in the high-stakes business

of toy design and manufacturing hadn't necessarily changed his attitude.

He picked up a four-layer chocolate cake for dessert and went through the checkout line.

His anger over Meg's deception was beginning to cool, if not his surprise at his own vulnerability to her ploy. He was usually smart where women were concerned, and after the experience with Jillian, he'd considered himself more vigilant than ever.

But Meg had sneaked beyond his barriers with those big blue eyes filled with her own vulnerability and the fear he occasionally glimpsed there. He'd been so busy trying to protect her from her own confusion that he'd forgotten to shield himself.

Now that he was thinking more clearly, he was sure she hadn't been acting all the time. He couldn't believe that trembling in another's arms could be staged—that one could fake the ignition of a kiss.

But then he asked himself how she could have real feelings for him and still keep the whole plan of this weeklong getaway a secret.

That's what you get, he told himself as he pocketed his change, *for having the arrogance to think that a beautiful woman would hand over ten thousand dollars for the pleasure of your company without an underlying motive.*

The supermarket doors opened for him and he walked out into frail sunshine. The rain had stopped, but the sky was an uncertain gray.

He was putting the groceries on the passenger seat of the Jeep when he saw the four men lined up at the end of the parking lot. He recognized two of them from that night in the underground parking structure in San Francisco and felt excitement rather than trepidation. He'd like very much to repay those two, and he had pent-up energy to expend from the fight Meg wouldn't give him this morning.

He faced them, feeling the supple strength in his body, the unimpassioned calm. Steadiness was a much better warring tool than anger. He took several steps toward them as they began to move toward him.

The two he remembered were very big, the third small but muscular, the fourth slight and scarred and reaching into his pocket for something.

Amos kept an eye on that one, determined not to let him get behind him. They began to spread out. Amos narrowed his concentration, deciding that the biggest ones looked the least intelligent and were probably the weakest link.

He was about to surprise them with an attack when he suddenly found himself looking at three very broad backs and one rather fragile one. He heaved a sigh of frustration. His bodyguards had found him.

MEG WAS EAGER TO MIX IT up with somebody, and she almost didn't care who. When the man at the far end of the lineup ran at Brian, she headed for one of the big ones in the middle, eager to wipe the look of stunned disbelief off his face.

He played right into her hands by punching out at her. She dodged, caught his wrist and used his weight and propulsion to toss him over her shoulder and onto his back.

He never even got up.

Ben and his opponent collided with her and knocked her off balance.

She scrambled to her feet again as the small, muscular guy came at her, but a pair of arms wrapped around her waist—a pair of arms she recognized instantly.

She braced for the assailant's blow, but it sailed harmlessly past her as the pair of arms holding her pulled her out of the way and dropped her aside. Amos danced forward with a right and the thug fell like a stone.

The rest of the confrontation was brief and swift, and in a moment Brian had a foot on his man's chest, Ben had a knee to another guy's back, and Frank took the guy Amos had decked by the shirt collar when he tried to struggle to his feet.

Brian waved at the group of people huddled together in the supermarket entrance. "Someone call the police!" he shouted.

An aproned man waved back and ran through the little crowd into the market.

Meg turned to Amos, prepared to give him a piece of her mind for taking her out of the battle, but he clearly had issues of his own.

"What are you guys?" he demanded of her brothers. "The bad half of the Magnificent Seven? I was handling myself."

Brian frowned at him. "You were outgunned."

"Oh, he's never outgunned," Meg put in, looking for an outlet for her exasperation with the lot of them. "He's big and bad because of a rough childhood and he isn't afraid of anything. He didn't need us. Or so he'd like to think.''

Amos turned on her. "Well, pardon me if I'm unwilling to be defended by a woman and a priest!''

"Hey!'' Frank protested. "Don't go feeling superior because I wear a collar.''

Amos gave him an impatient look. "That isn't what I meant. I don't question your ability, I just don't think you should have to exercise it on my behalf.''

"Oh, don't be so righteous!'' Meg rubbed a stiffness in her right shoulder. "You prevented me from doing my job! It isn't all about muscle, you know, it's about…''

"If you'd been that good at what you do,'' he interrupted, "I wouldn't have been able to move you, would I?''

"You…!'' She stopped herself just as she was about to explain how that had happened, realizing it wouldn't be a good thing to tell him. Not now. He'd been able to break her concentration because she'd recognized the touch as his. She'd lost focus and her professionalism had flown.

Two police cars—probably the only two in Bluebell Lake—rounded the corner into the parking lot, sirens blaring and lights flashing. Jillian's men were taken into custody and Meg and her brothers and Amos followed them to the police station.

A cheerful dispatcher stashed Amos's bag of groceries in the refrigerator for safekeeping while everyone answered questions and gave reports.

Meg waited with Amos on a wooden chair in a

small anteroom while the sheriff checked her brothers' credentials.

"I don't think you *are* rid of the death wish you had as a child," Meg said, legs crossed, arms folded, staring straight ahead at a bulletin board covered with a gun safety class schedule, a plea for volunteers for a community project involving baked goods, and numerous other notices whose type was too small for her to read. But she tried, just to avoid looking at Amos. "This refusal to have a bodyguard is reckless and foolish, and your taking off this morning was just plain childish."

"I'm better able to take care of myself than you give me credit for," he replied mildly. "And you could do with a little recklessness yourself, *Margaret.* You're even more protective of yourself than you are of your clients."

SHE TURNED TO HIM, icy disdain in her eyes. "I'd have thought convincing a stranger to spend a week with you in a cabin and seducing him would be considered recklessness extraordinaire."

He made a face at her. "I suppose it might have if any *real* seduction had taken place. We never got close to serious lovemaking, and every time we even turned in that direction, you backed out."

"I was supposed to be protecting you," she reminded him. "I couldn't afford the distraction."

"I think you were protecting yourself," he corrected her, "and you couldn't afford the risk. I think you're so used to your father and brothers looking after you that, though you make a point of fighting their protection all the time, when it comes to the crunch, you even protect yourself.''

"That's crazy."

"Yes," he agreed. "It is."

She gave him that look of displeased royalty again. "You believe my attentions to you were all made up for the purpose of keeping an eye on you, anyway. So, what does it matter how I acted, or what was self-protective and what wasn't?"

"No," he said. "I know you were falling in love with me. What I resent is that even though you were, you were still able to lie to me and deceive me. And I've had enough of that for one lifetime, thanks."

"Oh, spare me." She looked down at the foot she absently kicked forward and back. "I can't believe you didn't see that coming with Jillian. You were competitors in the same business, for heaven's sake. You're telling me it never occurred to you that she might be after something other than your charms? Even in matters of security, we look for trouble in the most obvious places."

"My trusting nature, I guess," he replied. "I didn't see through you, either. At least I'm accessible."

"Bully for you."

The sheriff arrested all four of Jillian's men for attempted assault.

Amos and Meg and her brothers went back to the cabin.

A YANKEES VERSUS Cardinals baseball game on television and a pan of nachos Ben and Amos put together seemed to nurture a growing camaraderie among her brothers and Amos. Meg couldn't understand why she resented it so much, unless it was that she was generally angry with all of them.

Brian called their father when they got home and Paul reported that Jillian had left her home in high dudgeon that afternoon and gone to the Mystic Spa. It was deduced that she had probably been her henchmen's one phone call and had needed a spa break to reduce the tension of having such inferior underlings.

"I think the heat's off temporarily," he said. "But stay alert."

Meg spent the afternoon reading in her room, trying to tune out the men's cheering and shouted strategies during the game.

Everyone helped with dinner. Ben made a salad, Brian sliced tomatoes, Frank scrubbed potatoes and put them in to bake, and Amos cooked steaks.

Meg, relegated once again to rookie duties, set the table and made coffee.

Brian raved over the steak. "I haven't had this in ages, except on the occasional client lunch when Jamie isn't there to monitor my red meat intake."

"Yeah," Ben agreed. "You can't even get a steak in a nice restaurant anymore. It's all chicken or seafood in sauces you've never heard of. And covered with hazelnuts. Why is that?"

"The parish would never be able to afford a budget for this kind of menu," Frank said, ignoring Ben's culinary philosophy. "This is a real treat for me."

"So, how serious are you two?" Ben asked, looking from Amos to Meg. "Any chance we're going to get Amos to cook like this for us on a regular basis?"

Brian put a hand over his eyes and Frank blessed himself.

Meg shook her head in disbelief. Amos smiled at her.

"What?" Ben asked. "They know we know something was going on. Why shouldn't we talk about it? If there's a problem, maybe we can help them fix it."

"Ben," Brian said, "you couldn't fix anything between a man and a woman if you had instructions and an assistant."

"We've decided we don't like each other after all," Meg put in, reaching over to pat Ben's hand. "You'll just have to cook for yourself, Ben. Or get Blitzen to do it for you."

"Bambi."

"Right."

"That's not entirely true." Amos took it upon himself to correct her. "I made it clear that I didn't like being lied to, and Meg decided that was narrow-minded of me."

She dropped her fork with a clatter. "You were lied to for your own good!"

Amos pointed calmly to her brothers. "They protect you for what they consider 'your own good.'" His quiet voice gave a slight emphasis to her words. "But you don't appreciate that."

"That's different!"

"How?"

"My children," Frank said with a theatrical raising of his hands, "I think that line of argument is futile. Let's put all this passion to work at Monopoly after dinner."

"I'll get coffee and dessert," Meg said, edgy and anxious, needing to move.

While she worked, Amos carried in plates and filled the dishwasher. She tried to ignore him as she poured the pot of coffee into a carafe, then made another pot.

Amos handed her dessert plates and forks. He seemed reluctant to give her the big knife. "Can I trust you with this in the mood you're in?"

"If I were prone to murder when I'm upset," she said, taking it from him, "my brothers would have died as children."

He got the dishwasher going, then came back to the table to pick up the plates, now bearing slices of rich chocolate cake.

She watched him walk away and stuck her tongue out at him. Unfortunately, he turned sideways to go through the doorway and glanced back just in time to catch her.

He shook his head and kept going.

Meg carried out the rest of the cake, then a tray with the carafe of coffee and five cups.

Frank set out the Monopoly game on the cleared table, and while they had their coffee and cake, they listened to the news. Meg had just returned from the kitchen with a fresh pot of coffee when Brian pointed at the television screen and gasped in disbelief, "It's Grandma."

Meg hurried over and stood between the chair where Brian sat and the sofa occupied by Ben, Frank and Amos. Sure enough, it was Grandma Rooney. She seemed to be at some sort of function in San

Francisco where she was being feted along with other philanthropic celebrities.

"Guinevere Rooney is well known for her generosity and fund-raising," the reporter said. He was a tall, handsome man who leaned protectively over the petite woman in a glittery red dress. Her white hair, thin but elegantly styled, framed a delicate face in which...

"Oh, my God!" Meg exclaimed as the camera closed in on her grandmother. Her doll's face filled the screen.

"That isn't...?" Brian began, leaning out of his chair for a closer look.

"It's a...ring!" Frank said. "Piercing her eyebrow!"

"Go Grandma!" Ben laughed.

"I understand," the reporter said, "that you're just back from Africa, where you were buying art?"

"I am," she confirmed, her voice high and a little shaky. "It's for the art museum in Shasta, California. I met my late husband in Shasta. It's special to me."

"Wonderful. Um...Mrs. Rooney." The reporter glanced at the camera with a smile. "I know the audience will be upset with me if I *don't* ask about the ring in your eyebrow."

She put a bony, arthritic finger to it and laughed. "Cool, isn't it? I have a friend who promised to match my donation if I did it."

"To the museum?"

"No, to a new center for the Wild Hills Community College's Women in Transition program."

Meg gasped and set the coffeepot down on the table before she dropped it.

"I'm establishing it in the name of my granddaughter, Margaret Guinevere Loria, on the occasion of her marriage to Amos Pike this coming Saturday."

Meg was vaguely aware of various exclamations of surprise from her brothers, and Amos's quick glance at her before a sudden roar in her ears took over and drowned out all other sounds.

As the room began to reel around her, she remembered Amos's observation about the speed of the earth's orbit and swore she could feel it moving under her. Hands caught her just as the floor fell away.

MARRIAGE TO AMOS PIKE.

Marriage to Amos Pike.

Marriage to Amos Pike.

Meg heard the words over and over like a repetitive mantra. She tried to make sense of it, but the world was hot and foggy and she didn't seem to be able to think.

A small breeze was providing some comfort, but her ears buzzed and she didn't think she could move.

"Meg?" a voice called, as though from far away. "Meg? Are you with me? Meg, come on!"

She opened her eyes very slowly to find herself being fanned by a folded newspaper, four faces leaning over her in concern. Her brothers and Amos.

She focused on Amos's face, the mantra ringing in her head once more—"Marriage to Amos..."

There was the soft ring of a cell phone and Brian backed away from the sofa to answer it.

"I'll get some water," Ben said.

Frank moved, too. "I'll get a blanket."

Meg put a hand to her head. "Amos," she said, almost afraid to ask. "Did I dream Grandma Rooney on the six o'clock news?"

Sitting on the edge of the sofa beside her, he tossed the newspaper onto the coffee table and patted her hand. "I'm afraid you didn't. How do you feel?"

"Horrible." She tried to sit up. He helped her and propped a few pillows behind her. "You hate me, right? Even more than you did before. I know, I know. Don't worry. I'll get it all..."

Frank returned with the blanket and draped it over her. Ben offered her a glass of water, which she accepted gratefully. She gulped it down and handed back the empty glass.

"So...we all heard it?" she asked the worried faces looking down on her.

Ben and Frank nodded. "Dad, too," Ben said. "He's on the phone with Brian."

"Ooh." Meg put a hand to her now-throbbing head. "How can you be smiling?" she asked Amos. "My grandmother just announced to several million people that you're marrying me on Saturday. I don't understand. She does get things confused, but usually it's things she knows that she just gets twisted around. I mean...she's never even *met* you. How would she...?"

"Actually," he said, readjusting her blanket when her fidgety movements made it slip, "she has." When her eyes widened in confusion, he explained. "I wasn't sure who she was when you were telling me about her, but when I saw her on the news, I recognized her. I heard she was donating one hundred Pickled Pepper polar bears to a children's hospital, so we gave them to her. She stopped by the office to thank me.'' He smiled. ''She kept calling me Andy. I assumed it was an Amos and Andy mix-up. Anyway, she said she wished she could fix me up with her granddaughter. I guess in her mind, she put the information together the way she wanted it.''

Meg couldn't see any humor in that. Her grandmother had confused her ex-fiancé with her current security client and told the nation they were getting married! That Saturday! She wanted to scream, but she was afraid to waste her breath, which was coming in shallow gasps.

Brian came to lean over the back of the sofa. ''How you doin', babe?'' he asked with a sympathetic smile. He held up the phone. ''It's Dad. He says Grandma's lawyer just called him because he couldn't reach you. He said he's transferring the money to the school in the morning. Dad heard the newscast, too. He wants to know if you want him to try to straighten Grandma out, or if you'd rather do it yourself. He says he knows you hate it when he interferes, but he can go to her in person and you can't. It might be hard to make her understand over the phone.''

Meg groaned. A million dollars for Becky's program down the tubes. Becky would be devastated when it turned out not to be true.

When she reached for the phone, Amos intercepted her, catching her hand. He looked up at Brian. ''Tell him she'll call him back in ten minutes.''

"What?" Meg asked.

"Ten minutes," he repeated to Brian.

Brian studied him one protracted moment, then put the phone to his ear and wandered away. "Dad..."

Amos looked at Ben and Frank hovering around the edge of the room. "Could you excuse us for a couple of minutes, please?"

"Sure." Frank caught Brian's elbow and drew him—still talking to their father—into the kitchen.

AMOS REALIZED THIS WAS his opportunity to find out if his relationship with Meg had all the potential he thought it did. Left to her own devices, Meg could withdraw for an entire lifetime, unconvinced of the growing love she felt for him and the sexual power she wielded.

"What are you thinking?" she asked, sitting up a little straighter.

"I'm thinking," he replied carefully, "that your grandmother's mistake can work to our benefit."

She stared at him, apparently trying to figure out how that could be and finally failing. "Amos, she just told half of the country that she's making a huge donation to my pet project because she thinks I'm marrying someone who really left me for someone else!"

"That's not entirely true," he reminded her. "She thinks you're marrying me."

"Because she has you confused with Daniel."

"Yes, but that doesn't really matter, does it? In her mind, she's connected you and me. So...let's connect."

She stared at him again, one complex emotion after

another chasing across her wide blue eyes. "You mean we should...?"

"Get married," he said, filling in for her. "Yes. Then your friend and her program will get the money."

Her thoughts finally seemed to come into focus and she shook her head emphatically. "I can't lie to my grandmother just to get what I want."

"That's where you're missing what's going on here," he said. He put a hand to the back of the sofa and looked into her eyes. "I don't think it's a lie, Meg."

"What do you mean?"

"We're very interested in each other, but the situation wouldn't allow a relationship to happen. You couldn't let yourself go, because you were guarding me and wanted to be vigilant. And I knew something was going on that I didn't understand, but I didn't know what. I think we need a chance to find out what's really between us without all the distractions."

She considered that with a frown. "But you said you didn't trust me because I had to lie to you to get you here. So...why would you want to marry me?"

He felt reasonably sure she'd never believe that he had fallen in love with her, so he had to come up with something else. Something she would find credible.

"All right," he said, looking her in the eye, "I think you owe me."

She held his gaze. "How so?"

"So far," he replied, "I've done all the work in this relationship. I worked hard to help you with everything you wanted to know about the man-woman dynamic. But most of what I got in return was interest, eager participation, and then—just about every time—your withdrawal and my frustration.''

She was following him; he could see it in her eyes. One moment they were turbulent with anger, the next a little dreamy with possibilities. She couldn't seem to decide which should dominate. She folded her arms atop the blanket.

''Are you telling me,'' she asked directly, ''that you're willing to marry me for a wedding night? For...sex?''

''That's the part we never got to,'' he said. ''And it's not sex, it's lovemaking. While it isn't everything in a relationship, it's a part that can sometimes smooth out the rest of it. It can give you a way to communicate that levels the court, pushes the grievances and the fears aside and lets you just be...the two of you.''

She studied him in puzzlement. ''If you understand that's how a relationship should be, then you must have had one.''

He shook his head. ''I just remember my parents. Two very happy, loving people. And though I didn't know then, of course, about the physical side of their relationship, it was hard to miss their pleasure in each other. I haven't had that. But I've been looking for it.''

Her expression softened, as though she were seeing the same picture of her parents that he was of his. Then her eyes became apologetic and she glanced toward the kitchen to make sure her brothers were still out of earshot.

"Amos, remember when you asked me if I was a virgin?" she asked urgently.

He laughed. "Ticked you off, as I recall."

"Because it's practically true." She waved a hand in the direction of the kitchen. "As a teenager, they were always hovering, and in college I never had the...the confidence in myself as a woman that appeals to guys. And, my being skilled in martial arts puts a lot of them off."

"That was then," he said.

"Yeah, well...Daniel was my first. My only." She played with the fringe on the blanket Frank had put over her, then looked up at Amos, her eyes troubled. "I thought I loved him, and yet when it came to lovemaking, I didn't really...like it. I mean, I know it's not like the ecstasy you see in the movies, but I thought there was more to it than that, you know?"

Yeah, he was beginning to think he did. "Did Daniel like it?"

She shrugged. "He never said, and it was all over faster than I'd expected, so it was hard to tell." She smiled thinly. "I think the real clue is that he left me for an older woman."

"The only thing that clue reveals," he said, shaking his head at her, "is that Daniel was a jerk. You'd like it with me, Meg."

MEG HAD ABSOLUTELY NO doubt about that. She was even able to smile at the thought. "I'm sure I would," she said. But it wasn't herself she was worried about. At least, not in regard to making love with him. "But you're after something so special, Amos. What if you don't find it…with me?''

"I don't think that would happen," he said. "But we have to be practical. We'll get married, your friend will get her money, and we'll see if what we have together is worth a lifetime. If it isn't, you're free to go. Or I am."

It sounded altogether too practical. She remembered how happy her parents had been together, and how much Brian and Jamie loved each other.

"It almost seems like a crime," she said, her eyes focused on a distant memory of her mother, "to plan to take vows to love each other while building in an escape.''

He nodded. "But I think the situation allows us a few foibles.''

She wanted to let herself love Amos Pike more than she wanted anything. But how would she be able to go on if Amos couldn't love her? It was more than simple pride involved now. During the few days they'd spent together, she'd found his company amusing, entertaining and stimulating. And she'd found herself trying to give that back.

She'd practically forgotten Daniel, except for the residual concerns about her own sexuality with which their relationship had left her.

Brian peered around the corner of the kitchen, clearing his throat. "Pardon me, guys, but Dad's holding. Should I tell him you need more time and you'll call him back?"

Meg looked at Amos.

Amos looked at Meg.

"You want to take this reckless ride with me?" he asked.

It suddenly seemed like a brilliant idea. She might want to change her mind later, but she wasn't going to make her decision based on fears and nebulous concerns.

"Yes," she said firmly.

Amos stood and went to take the phone from Brian. "Mr. Loria?" he said, coming back to the sofa. Meg tossed the blanket aside and swung her legs over so he could sit beside her. "Amos Pike, here. I'd like to ask for your daughter's hand in marriage."

Frank and Ben wandered out of the kitchen to flank Brian, who now stared at them from the middle of the room.

"Yes, I know. No, it's more than the money, although I'm sure that's affecting Meg's decision. But we've enjoyed the time we've spent together and think maybe your mother-in-law's mistake might be a good thing all around. Of course. She's right here."

Amos handed Meg the phone.

"Hi, Dad," she said, a swell of excitement filling her chest. "The wedding's going to go ahead as planned."

"Meggie," he said, his voice mingling surprise and concern. "Are you sure about this? I mean, Daniel just abandoned you, and you've known Amos Pike less than a week—and under circumstances that can sometimes confuse proximity with love. Marriage lasts a lifetime, you know. Or, at least, it's supposed to."

"We've made a contingency plan," she explained.

"Love is not supposed to need a contingency plan."

"Amos thinks that our unusual circumstances allow for a few foibles."

"Meg…"

"Trust me, Dad," she said. "You and the boys have spent my whole life running in to back me up, so that at the ripe old age of twenty-six I'm not even sure what I'm capable of."

"If you're doing this just to prove to me…"

"Dad, I'm doing it to prove something to me. But I'd really like to do it with your blessing."

She heard a groan and could imagine him rubbing his eyes as he wrestled with a problem that required trust rather than security. "All right. You have it. But if you remember, your wedding was scheduled for Saturday morning and the toy show's also on Saturday."

"Oh-oh." She held the phone to her chest and relayed the message to Amos. "We could change the date, but Grandma Rooney announced it on television."

"What time was the wedding scheduled?"

"Eight-thirty in the morning."

He nodded. "That'll work. The show doesn't open until noon, and all the big stuff happens on Sunday, anyway. But I guess that'll mess up the reception."

"Who needs a reception?" She repeated the information to her father. "Dad, can you rebook the church for me, please? All the reception stuff's canceled, so we'll just leave that because there won't be time."

"You want me to call all the guests and tell them they're reinvited?"

"Please. Just be sure to tell them no gifts and no reception."

"Got it."

"Thanks, Dad. I love you, even if you don't trust me to do my job, and even if I did quit this morning when I thought I was talking to you and it turned out to be Jamie."

"Yes," he replied dryly. "She told me. You called me a pimp or something, and claimed to have lost faith in me as a parent."

Meg could imagine Jamie taking a certain pleasure in repeating the words. She'd always taken Meg's side against the Loria men's compulsive protection. "I did *not* call you a pimp. I said you'd used me as a call girl to get Amos here rather than as a bodyguard. When it came to the real work, you sent in the boys. That wasn't fair."

Amos wrinkled his brow at her words. She erased them with a wave of her hand.

Her father was silent for a moment, then he said, albeit with a trace of insincerity, "I'm sorry. It's hard to think of you being as tough as they are."

"Well, I can be. Anyway, you've just restored my faith in you as a father. What's new on Jillian? Has she hired another complement of goons?"

"Not to my knowledge. She just seems to be sulking. But we're still watching her every move."

"Then it's safe to bring Amos home?"

"We'll have him so well-covered, *you* won't even

be able to get through. Don't worry. Everything will be fine. Now, let me talk to Brian.''

"Okay. Bye, Dad." Meg held the phone out. "Brian, Dad wants you."

Brian came to take the phone and walked away with it. Meg was alone on the sofa with Amos. She looked into his handsome, intelligent face and felt a momentarily disabling sense of unreality.

Meg Loria, near virgin, was marrying Amos Pike, darling of San Francisco's most discerning socialites?

He grinned. "You look a little like you did the day you got the fishhook in your finger. Do you feel caught? In pain?"

She realized that she didn't feel trapped at all. And there was no pain. Just excitement and a rising sense of hope and promise.

"I'm happy," she said honestly. "Mostly, I've enjoyed our time together. But are you really sure you want to do this?"

"I'm sure."

"You don't find marriage a little intimidating?"

He grinned. "I'm fearless, remember?"

CHAPTER TEN

AMOS GOT UP AT 2:00 A.M. after three hours of staring into the darkness of his room. He remembered seeing a bottle of brandy in one of the upper kitchen cupboards and thought a few good swigs might help him relax.

He couldn't quite believe Meg had agreed to his plan. Of course, the wedding hadn't happened yet, and she had a record for backing out on him where matters of the heart were concerned. But this was also a matter of money for a program she really believed in, so that might make the difference if she was tempted to change her mind. Amos didn't know what he would do if that happened. He truly believed that he and Meg were meant to be together.

Groping his way into the kitchen, he tried to find the brandy without putting on the light. If memory served, the squat brown bottle was behind the box of pancake mix, but in front of the...

"Where do you think you're going?" a testy voice demanded.

Amos's heart rattled in his chest as the light went on and something fell out of the cupboard at him. He juggled the bottle of brandy and finally caught it, a hand to his pounding heart. Brian stood in the open

doorway to the backyard, an underarm holster unbut-
toned on his left side.

Amos was more surprised than annoyed. Spreading
his arms to indicate his bare chest and sweat bottoms,
he held up the brandy. "Do I look like I'm going
somewhere?"

"It's one o'clock in the morning," Brian said.

"I know. I couldn't sleep so I got up to..." Before
he could explain further, Ben burst in from the living
room, a pistol held out in front of him and steadied
in the palm of his other hand.

He took in the tableau, then slipped his gun into a
holster identical to Brian's. "I thought I heard a scuffle," he explained. Then he smiled from one man to
the other. "What's going on? Are we having a brandy
break?"

Stepping into the room, Brian closed the outside
door behind him. "I guess Amos is," he said, coming
toward the table. "I thought he might be *making* a
break."

Ben frowned. "What do you mean?"

Amos pulled down three juice glasses and carried
them and the brandy to the table. He went back for
two more when Frank appeared in the doorway, followed by Meg.

She came around Frank, gun held out just as Ben
had done. Then, seeing only her brothers and Amos,
she rolled her eyes and turned to Frank. "You know,
when I'm the one who's armed, it works better if I'm
out in front."

"I'm armed with prayer," he said with a grin.

She put the gun away in the same kind of holster

her brothers wore. It was strapped over the short-sleeved pink sweatshirt she'd worn to bed with matching shorts. Amos found the picture incongruous. "Prayer doesn't make you bulletproof, you know. If it did, all the saints would still be alive."

Once he'd put the brandy and extra glasses down, Amos pulled out a chair. "I feel like I'm here with the Mafia," he said. "You guys wear those all the time?"

"It's important not to get lazy," Brian said. "That's why we posted guards tonight. Dad thinks Jillian's just pouting, but who knows for sure. She might have hired someone else." He smiled suddenly. "Now that you're going to be our brother-in-law, we have to keep you safe."

Amos pinned Brian with a look. "And prevent me from making a break." He sat down in the chair, then drew Meg onto his knee while her brothers occupied the other seats. "If we're going to be friends," he added, looking at each one in turn, "don't mistake me for Daniel, all right? I never walk away from a promise."

"Good." Brian poured the brandy and passed glasses around the table. "Because we won't ever let Meg be hurt like that again. And you have to admit that this wedding after just four days is a lit-tle…unusual."

Amos had to grant them that. "But so is the situation your father and your sister led me into." He gave Meg a censorious look.

She met it without flinching. "It was to keep you safe," she said simply. Then she smiled at her brothers. "Don't worry. I've given him a pretty hard time and he's taken it very well. I also decked him once when I mistook him for one of Jillian's men, so he knows what I can do."

Brian held up his glass. "Dad just wanted us to try to assess whether or not he'd be good for you."

"As opposed to trusting my own assessment?"

"I'm sure your father was just wanting some assurance that you were thinking clearly," Amos said, patting her hip. "He's just doing his job."

Frank sipped at his brandy, then smiled. "Meg gets testy about Dad because she thinks she's the only one of us that he watches like a hawk. But he's called my bishop a few times to make sure someone's keeping an eye on me. The school's in a pretty unsavory neighborhood."

"My landlady is his secretary's grandmother," Ben said with an exasperated sigh, "so he knows every move I make, too."

"Me, too." Brian finished his brandy. "He has my wife wrapped around his little finger. Her father's gone so she's adopted him. I'm afraid his benevolent input into your affairs is going to come with your marriage to Meg."

Amos nodded. "I grew up most of my life without a father. I think you're all pretty lucky." He looked around the table at the holsters. "I'm going to feel really guilty if you all have to stay up and watch over me."

"Actually, we're just about to change shifts," Brian said, looking at his watch. "Ben and I had ten to two. Meg and Frank have two to six."

Amos opened his mouth to protest Meg's sitting up to guard him, but she pointed a finger at him and fixed him with a firm look. "Don't even think about objecting. It's my *job*."

He changed his approach. "I wasn't going to."

She narrowed her eyes suspiciously. "You were, too."

"No," he denied innocently. "I was just going to tell you that I'll sit up with you."

She closed her eyes, then opened them again. "Amos, I'm sitting up to *protect* you. That means you have to stay inside with Ben and Brian."

He shook his head. "No, it doesn't. You've just accepted my proposal of marriage. My place is wherever you are."

"But I'll be right outside."

"So will I."

Apparently at a loss for words, she turned to Brian. "Don't you have anything to say?" she asked. "Tell him the client doesn't sit on guard duty with the bodyguard."

Brian sent Amos a grinning glance, then shook his head at Meg. "I thought you considered this your operation. You don't like it when I interfere."

"He can sit with me," Frank said in all apparent innocence. "I'd like to get to know him better, anyway."

Meg shook her head. "You'll be praying while you're watching. I want him to have someone's undivided attention."

Frank shrugged. "Then he is better off with you."

She looked around the table and accepted that she'd

been had. "How did they indoctrinate you so fast?" she asked Amos.

Brian pushed away from the table with a stretch. "We're four of a kind, I guess."

"That's good if you're playing poker," she grumbled, getting to her feet as Amos and everyone else at the table stood.

"Come on." Ben kissed her cheek and headed off to bed. "We're great however you look at it!"

Once Brian said good-night and Frank went to take his post in front of the house, Meg caught her hair into a bunch at the back of her head and dug into her shorts pocket for the clip. "Okay," she said, as though she were granting him royal dispensation, "but you have to cooperate."

"Sure," he agreed, following her to the door. She stopped with her hand on the knob and looked up into his eyes. "And no touching me or kissing me."

"At all?"

"At all. We're going to keep our eyes open and talk about mundane things like weather and politics. Stuff like that. Things that won't distract me."

"I understand."

"All right." She pulled the back door open and turned off the kitchen light. They sat side by side on the small bench on the back porch in the balmy Wyoming night.

"Think it's going to snow?" he asked gravely.

She backhanded him in the gut.

PAUL LORIA PULLED UP to the rose-bordered side entrance of St. Philip's Catholic Church and groaned.

Jamie, sitting beside him in pale yellow chiffon, said gravely, "Oh-oh."

"What?" Meg leaned over the front seat to look out.

"Press photographers." Becky Winston, also in yellow chiffon, pointed to a television news truck. "TV and newspaper, it looks like. Is that bad for security?"

"No," Meg replied, leaning back in her seat. "It's probably good. Jillian has too much at stake financially and otherwise to try to hurt Amos in front of so many witnesses."

"I don't know," Jamie said. "Crazy people are unpredictable."

"She isn't crazy, she's greedy," Meg corrected her.

"I hope you're right."

"I don't think we're going to get in without you having to talk to somebody," Meg's father said. "Are you okay with that, or do you want me to get the boys?"

"I think you should let the press see you," Jamie said, turning to her with a bright smile. She was a petite blonde, yet Meg knew Brian was putty in her hands. "You look sensational."

Meg had exchanged the formal lace-and-ruffles wedding dress in which she'd planned to marry Daniel and bought a short sheath made of white beaded lace with a low neckline formed by a wide bow six inches deep. Another wide bow was fitted atop her upswept hair, and a little chin-length veil covered her face.

The problem was solved a moment later when Brian and Ben came out, backed by six other young men Meg didn't recognize.

"Who are they?" she asked no one in particular.

"They work for Amos," her father replied with a glance at her in the rearview mirror. When she expressed surprise that he knew that, he added with a sly smile, "I've been checking him out. I recognize two of the faces. Get ready. It looks like they're going to form a wedge to get you inside. Your fiancé was thinking, Meggie. I like that."

Grandma Rooney and Elizabeth Day, her companion, were waiting for Meg in the alcove in the vestibule where the bride waited to go down the aisle. She looked vibrant and happy in a chic pink suit as she wrapped Meg in a fragrant embrace.

"I have dreamed of this day!" she said, primping the bow at Meg's neckline. "You look beautiful. Just like your mother did on her wedding day. And Lizzie, here, thought I was mistaken about your groom." She jerked a thumb in the direction of her companion, who gave Meg a rueful shrug. "I know I sometimes get things confused, but who could be wrong about a wonderful man like Andy."

Meg knew her father had spoken to Lizzie the night of the mix-up and explained the decision to proceed with the wedding—with another groom.

"Amos," Lizzie corrected her.

"Amos," Grandma repeated dutifully. "He says I can visit the two of you whenever I want."

Meg blinked at her. "You've seen him?"

"Of course I've seen him. He and your brothers picked Lizzie and me up and brought us to the church!"

Meg looked to Lizzie for confirmation and got it in a subtle nod.

"Well." Grandma hugged her again. "We have to go. I'm being mother of the bride today, remember, so I have to be ready to make my appearance. Good luck, dear."

Lizzie let Guinevere get a few steps ahead of her, then leaned toward Meg and said in a whisper, "Amos is a much better choice for you, Meggie, than that Daniel person we met at Easter. Good work."

Everyone liked her fiancé, Meg noted as she walked up the aisle of a packed church on her father's arm. Amos's side was as full as hers, though he was not the groom mentioned on the invitations. This was even weirder than *The Philadelphia Story*, where one groom was replaced with another at the last moment.

As Becky and Jamie took their places to the left of the altar, Meg saw Amos waiting for her, Brian and Ben lined up behind him. They looked wonderful—formal replicas of their casual selves.

Frank stood in the middle at the top of the carpeted steps, in a white-and-gold vestment. He'd arranged to have the church's prerequisite marriage classes waived so that Amos and Meg could be married immediately. He smiled at his sister as she approached.

Her father stopped at the head of the aisle and tucked her arm into Amos's.

And then everything seemed to fly at fast-forward

speed. She was aware of every single step in the nuptial mass, committed to memory every word spoken, every movement made, the touch of Amos's hands on hers as he repeated the vows and slipped the ring on her finger.

Then she found her voice just when she'd become so sure this was all too unreal for her to have one. But there it was, audible and clear.

"You may kiss the bride," Frank said, and she watched Amos's mouth come toward hers as though in slow motion. Despite his claim that their marriage allowed for a contingency plan, the touch of his lips was confident and possessive.

Then triumphant organ music began and she walked down the aisle with Amos—a married woman.

Her father had arranged for cake and coffee to be served in the church hall next door, since there was still two hours before the opening of the toy show. Her "no gifts" decree had been ignored, and mounds of presents rose above and below a large table against the wall.

The press was kept away, but cameras were still very much in evidence. Lizzie had a video camera and Grandma Rooney followed her around, giving her directions like a small, gravelly voiced Spielberg.

Amos introduced Meg to his friends and his staff, including Jeannette Boradino and her son, Kyle.

"Actually, Jeannette and I are acquainted," Meg said.

He was surprised for a moment, then nodded knowingly. "*Jeannette* hired Loria Security?"

"I'm not fired again, am I?" Jeannette asked.

He put an arm around her shoulders. "Hardly. Remind me to give you a bonus. I said I didn't want a bodyguard, but I didn't know it would look like Meg."

"Bodyguard, huh?" Kyle Boradino, a twelve-year-old in a blue blazer over white slacks, eyed Meg skeptically. "You're very pretty, but you don't look like you could stop a punch."

"That's a mistake a lot of people make," she replied. "That's why I'm really good at it."

"So you say."

Meg resisted the impulse to toss the boy onto his back.

"I've seen her in action," Amos said. "I'd believe her if I were you."

Kyle smiled up at Amos politely. "I don't have to believe anything if I don't want to. Excuse me. I'd like some more punch." He started to walk away.

"Hey!" Amos caught a fistful of the shoulder of his blazer and pulled him back.

Kyle looked up at Amos in wide-eyed uncertainty.

"Maybe your mother would like some, too," Amos suggested.

Meg guessed that Kyle was considering ignoring Amos, then decided against it. Wisely, she imagined.

"Mom?" Kyle asked.

"Yes," she replied. "I'd love some punch. Thank you."

Amos let him go. The boy made a production of straightening his jacket with a resentful look over his shoulder, then headed for the punch bowl.

Jeannette groaned. "I hope he grows up before I kill him. I apologize. I made him promise he'd be polite, but I forgot to include civil. He's the world's biggest skeptic because his father made all kinds of promises to him that he didn't keep, and then he left us. Kyle is half me, so I live in hope that one day he'll stop behaving like the jerk his father was, but so far, it isn't happening."

Meg patted her hand. "I'm sure it will. Actually, he needs a couple of weeks with my father. Smart mouths weren't tolerated at our house, though my brothers tried hard."

Jeannette's eyes scanned the crowd and rested on Paul Loria, who was walking the perimeter of the room with a seemingly casual air. Meg knew he was taking in everything, double-checking, assessing.

Judging by her expression, Jeannette seemed less interested in what he was doing than in the man himself. A small smile erased her tight-lipped worry and she turned back to Meg with an embarrassed little tilt of her head.

"Your father spent some time with us while the two of you were at the cabin," she said, "keeping us apprised of how things were going. Kyle didn't make him very welcome. I'm sure the last thing Paul would want is to spend more time with him."

Jeannette spoke the words with real regret, as though more time spent with Meg's father was something she would look forward to.

Just before noon, Meg's family drove her and Amos to the Fulton Towers Hotel across the street from the convention center where the toy show was

being held. Amos had told her he'd booked rooms for
the weekend.

"Rooms" turned out to be two large suites that
took up an entire wing of the top floor, one for the
two of them, the other for her father and brothers,
who would continue to provide security until after the
show.

Meg stood in the middle of a high-ceilinged room
painted a soft blue and trimmed with gilt rococo em-
bellishments.

"Good grief!" she exclaimed, gaping like a hay-
seed.

Amos pushed her toward the bedroom, where their
luggage had been placed. "French provincial, I think.
Tends to be showy. Come on. I hate for my first husbandly duty to be to hurry you up, but we have to
pick up the prototype and we should be at the show
when the first visitors walk in."

"Right." She pulled off the bow in her hair and
opened her suit bag, looking for a blue dress Becky
had lent her.

Amos slipped off his jacket and shirt and pulled on
a dark blue polo shirt with his company's signature
polar bear in the logo on the pocket. He frowned at
Meg from across the bed.

"Are you going to regret this later?" he asked.
"The small reception, I mean. And having to spend
the afternoon of your wedding day at a toy show with
security all over the place."

She was surprised that he thought she might. She
was just so thrilled to have found him. But she didn't
want to sound needy by admitting that. "Of course

not. I'm sure it's just all part of the 'foibles' we're allowed.''

He came around the bed and took her face in his hands. His eyes were grave. "You're very undemanding, aren't you?"

She swept a hand around the opulent room. "Well, I'd complain about the unsatisfactory accommo—"

He cut her off with a kiss that destroyed the previous effort he'd made to hurry her. It was slow and thorough and made her feel as though every bone in her body had turned to fettuccini.

"If you'd be content to live in poverty," he said into her ear as he nuzzled it, "we'll just chuck the show and spend all weekend in this bed."

She trembled at the thought, anticipation and trepidation warring inside her. "Works for me," she said in a voice that was barely there. "I'm used to a much lower standard of living."

For a moment, she thought he might do just as he'd suggested. Then he groaned and straightened and turned her around to unzip her dress. "No," he said thoughtfully. "I'm thinking we should have four kids and they should all go to Harvard. For that we have to make some practical decisions."

She was both relieved and disappointed. "I like the idea, but are you grooming them to take over the toy company," she teased, carrying the blue dress into the bathroom, "before they're even a gleam in your eye?"

"You haven't been watching," he called after her. "The gleam's been in my eye since the day you bought me."

She leaned out of the bathroom with a finger to her lips. "Promise me you won't tell our children that."

He laughed. "Not a chance. It'll be my favorite story."

MEG WAS A LITTLE SURPRISED when Amos asked her father to drive them to the offices of Pike's Pickled Pepper Toy Company, an old three-story structure that looked as though it might have once been a mill.

"You hid the prototype in your office?" she asked. "I thought someone had rifled it twice already."

"They had," Amos replied. "That's why it seemed like a good idea. They'd been there and found nothing, so it might not occur to them to try a third time."

"Clever," she praised him.

Her father asked Frank and Ben to stay in the car and posted Brian just inside the front door. "Where are we going for the prototype?" Paul asked.

"It's in my office." Amos led the way to an elevator and pushed the third-floor button. They stepped out onto silver-gray carpet in a white corridor decorated with framed children's artwork.

Meg exclaimed over the pictures as she and her father followed Amos down the hall.

"They're from a contest we have in the schools every year," Amos explained. "Aren't they great? Winners get the toys of their choice. Here we are."

Meg was happy to see that his office was a little chaotic. It was also white, with lots of natural light, and the walls were covered with more children's artwork and past toy-show posters. A worktable against one wall was littered with plans and notes and construction materials.

"This drives Jeannette crazy," he said, heading across the room to what Meg guessed was intended to be a conversation corner. Two chairs and a small sofa were grouped around a square oak cube that probably served as a coffee table. "But I don't let anyone clean in here. I sometimes make notes on whatever I can find, and I'd hate to lose a great idea or a solution to a pesky design problem because it was mistaken for trash."

As he spoke, he carefully lifted up the cube, revealing another oak cube that held the space station prototype and a manila envelope that likely held the plans.

Paul leaned over to examine the toy. "Will you look at that. I can't imagine what it must be like to be a kid today with all this technology and all you geniuses figuring out ways for them to have fun."

Meg smiled at his fascination. "Is he going to have to bring one home for you, Dad?"

Her father straightened. "I think I deserve some reward for being the man who found you for him, or him for you, however you want to look at it."

"And maybe you should be rewarded," a voice said from the doorway of the adjoining office, "for finding what we've been looking for, too."

They turned to see two men filling the doorway. One of them held a pugnacious-looking Kyle Boradino by the arm. From the hallway opposite came two other men. After stepping into Amos's office, they quietly closed the door.

CHAPTER ELEVEN

MEG QUICKLY REVIEWED her options, but a gun held in close proximity to a twelve-year-old boy eliminated most of them. She recognized the men as the four who'd attacked Amos in the parking lot of the market in Bluebell Lake. The two big ones were brothers named Jekel. She couldn't remember their first names, but there was a blond one and a dark one. The small, square man was Lejewski, and the scarred one, Peterson.

"Kyle!" Amos said, taking a step toward the boy. The blond Jekel put a bullet in the chamber of his gun and pointed it at Amos. "Don't," he said.

"Don't point that at me." Amos slapped aside the hand that held the gun, took the boy and pushed him toward Meg.

Meg's heart lodged in her throat when Jekel recovered from his shock and pointed the pistol at Amos's temple.

"Tough guy, aren't you?" he said, an ugly sneer twisting his face. "You thought you were rid of us, but here we are. For a small price, a little paperwork got lost in the sheriff's office in Bluebell, and me and my friends are free men."

Meg sat the boy in a chair and looked at her father,

trying to guess what his intentions were. But he wouldn't meet her eyes. That meant he didn't have a plan and was coasting until an opportunity presented itself.

She could usually be calm in such circumstances. For all their volatility with one another, the Lorias had nerves of steel in a showdown. But a showdown had never involved the man she loved with a gun to his head. Though she tried to present a calm appearance for Kyle's sake and the ultimate outcome of this little scene, inside she was blithering.

Amos pointed to the space station, now visible in the open cube. "There's the game, for all the good it'll do you at this point. The show opens in half an hour. Do you really think you can copy it in that amount of time? Or pass it off as your own when I've had all the advance publicity?"

"It ain't about the game anymore," the dark-haired Jekel said, coming toward Meg. He walked around her, then stopped in front of her to look into her eyes. "This is personal. This chick here kicked me and knocked me down. I didn't like that. I didn't like it at all."

"Want to see me do it again?" she asked.

He caught her throat in his meaty hand. That was all she needed. With his middle vulnerable, she punched hard right in his gut. He doubled over and she brought her knee up under his chin.

At the same moment, Amos drove an elbow into the other Jekel's side, while Paul got Lejewski's jaw with a right cross.

Peterson, however, stopped the action with a revolver pointed at Kyle.

"Stop!" he shouted, his voice and his hands trembling. "Or I'll shoot the kid, I swear it."

Meg estimated the distance, figured she had the advantage of his nervousness, and sent a well-aimed kick sideways. The gun flew out of his hand and landed harmlessly behind him. Amos knocked him unconscious and retrieved the gun. Paul called the police.

Meg went to Kyle, who sat deep in one of the chairs, his eyes wide. "Are you all right?" she asked. "What were you doing here? How did they find you?"

"I was just looking around," he said, sitting up. His fear seemed to be receding and he looked as though he didn't quite believe what had happened. "I wasn't going to take anything, I just wanted to look at stuff."

Amos joined them and sat opposite him. "How'd you get in, Kyle?"

"Huh? Oh. My mom's key. She's working at the show and I knew she wouldn't miss it. I'm supposed to be at a friend's house." He looked from Amos to Meg, then over at Paul, who was still on the phone. "I can't believe you guys. It was like Nash Bridges or something!" He frowned at Meg. "You punched one guy out and kicked the gun right out of the other guy's hand. That was awesome!"

"Thank you." Meg pretended to take a bow. "But how'd you get here?"

Kyle frowned at the question. "On the bus. When

you don't have a driver's license, there's not a lot of choice." Then he focused on Amos. "And you're always duded up in a suit, but you dropped those two guys like you had a hammer!"

Meg saw Amos resist a smile. "I'm glad you're impressed. But why aren't you at your friend's house? Your mom doesn't know you're here, does she?"

Meg's brothers appeared and positioned themselves around the room to watch the thugs, who were just beginning to stir.

"I came because I like it here." His episode as a captive seemed to have blunted his ill temper. "I mean, it's full of toys." He indicated the high shelf that ran all around the office with samples of old and new toys. "And they're not for little kids. You have to have a brain to use the Knight's Journey and the Professor's Game."

"Thanks," Amos said. "Those are my designs, you know."

"I know!" Kyle's eyes grew even wider. "I mean, you're like this brain geek, but you got a punch like Holyfield!"

Amos raised an eyebrow. "Brain geek?"

"Smart," Kyle translated. "I thought if I came, I might see the space station." He leaned forward eagerly to peer into the cube at the game. "And there it is! I know nobody's supposed to know about it, but that day when we didn't have school for the teachers' meeting and Mom brought me here, you'd left the plan on your desk and I saw it. It's *so* cool."

"I'm glad you like it. But there's a basic rule even adults have to follow about being where you're supposed to be. What if your mom called your friend's house to see how you were doing and found out you never showed up there? She'd be frantic. Do you have your friend's number? What's his name?''

"Brad," Kyle told him. "Brad Johnston." He frowned. "His life is so perfect, you know. He has a mom who doesn't have to go to work, and a dad who comes home every night and really likes Brad and his brother. My life isn't like that. Mom's great, but my dad didn't like me, so he left.''

Meg's father sat on the arm of the sofa. "Your dad didn't leave because he didn't like you," he said. "Your mom told me he left because he lost his job and didn't know how to cope. It's hard to fail in front of your kid."

Kyle shook his head. "You don't understand, because you like your kids, too. My dad never liked me. I tried to make friends with him, but usually…he just made believe I wasn't there. I wouldn't care, only Mom has to work hard because he's gone.''

"She works hard," Amos corrected her, "because she's wild about you and wants you to have good opportunities and experiences."

Kyle smiled thinly but fondly. "I know. But she gets a little freaky about it." He grimaced. "She's making me go to this dance class where you have to eat at this fancy table and use the right fork, then ask a *girl* to dance!''

Amos laughed. "Well, if you have to dance, I'd take a girl as a partner over a guy."

"They're not as heavy when they step on your feet," Paul added.

Kyle studied Paul as though seeing him for the first time. "You were pretty good for an old guy," he said. "And you own this bodyguard company, so you, like, do this all the time?"

Paul seemed surprised by the praise and considered his answer. "Not *all* the time. At least half the time, the bad guy gives up easily. You just never know when that's going to happen. Excuse me." He stood and moved several steps away as his cell phone rang. He reached into his pocket to answer it.

"Hi, Jea— Yeah, I…no, he's…" Frantic conversation could be heard on the other end of the line. Paul tried interrupting several times, but when that failed, he said loudly, "Jenny!" That seemed to work, and he continued in a softer voice. "He's not missing. He's right here. Yeah. Well, it's a long story. Here, I'll let you talk to him."

AMOS, KYLE AND THE LORIAS were three hours late getting to the show. Gossip had apparently circulated about the reason for their tardiness and they were greeted with great excitement by the press and the other participants in the show. Since Amos had also gotten married that morning, he was viewed as a cross between Gipetto and the Renaissance Man.

The space station was greeted with excitement, amazement and giddy praise. Amos demonstrated it with an easy wit that made hard information digestible. He called Kyle in to help him show how a young person could use it with his computer.

Meg watched the demonstration and was as mesmerized as everyone else. Probably more so, she thought with a private grin, because she was going back to the hotel room with the brain geek tonight.

The Lorias had done well by their client today, and she'd contributed her share. She felt good about herself and positive about her life in general.

They were ready to leave the center when Jillian Chambers suddenly approached their booth. There hadn't been much action at hers, Meg had noticed as she'd done a circuit of the room. Jillian wore designer coveralls with the Chayco logo on them and came to Amos with her hand extended.

He took it.

Meg watched, ready to kick the woman senseless if necessary.

"I wanted to tell you there are no hard feelings," Jillian said with a seemingly genuine smile. "Some unfortunate misunderstandings have taken place between us, but I wanted you to know that I had nothing whatsoever to do with what happened this afternoon. I employed those men while I was in Wyoming for the auction. They were supposed to buy cattle for me for my place in Hidden Valley, but they tried to gain favor—and bonuses, I imagine—by trying to get you and secure the plans for the space station." She gave a convincing impression of being shocked and distressed. "When I heard what happened today, I asked my lawyer to go down to the police station to find out what it was all about. He said they were just out for revenge because you and Meg's family beat them at their own game in Bluebell Lake. Well, I'm sorry it happened. And on your wedding day."

Meg heard the slightest of sour notes in those last

few words and attributed it to Jillian having to put a good face on finally losing an old flame. She wasn't sure she could have done any better.

"We've made such a poor showing today," she said, "that I'm not even opening the booth tomorrow. We're going home tonight. I think I'll reevaluate and consider if it's even worth competing with you anymore. I just keep doing old favorites, but you've always got a new idea. Maybe I'll just retire with those cows."

Jillian gave Amos a quick hug, shook Meg's hand and wished her well, then walked out of their lives.

AMOS WATCHED JILLIAN GO, thinking that had been a sterling performance. But he knew that woman, and he couldn't see her ever giving up on anything. He also couldn't see her cheerfully taking second place to anyone, so maybe that little speech had been more genuine than he thought. The space station had been an even bigger hit than he'd hoped, and Chayco had apparently expended more effort on securing his designs than developing their own. Their offering of a Space Walker Wendy Doll with an interplanetary wardrobe hadn't made much of an impression on buyers or visitors.

"Do you believe her?" Meg asked as she shouldered her purse.

Slipping an arm around her, he led her toward the door. "I was just having that argument with myself. She'd never be content playing second fiddle to anyone, but on the other hand, she's a sore loser. So, I don't know. And frankly, tonight I don't care. I'm buying you dinner and taking you to bed.''

He should have known it wouldn't be that simple with the Lorias determined to protect him. Brian, Jamie, Frank and Ben had dinner several tables away in the hotel's dining room. Paul, Jeannette and Kyle occupied another table nearby.

"Why are they still here?" he asked Meg. "We got the space station safely to the show."

She smiled sympathetically. "Well, now you're family, so you no longer control your own life. As long as my father thinks you need protection, one of my brothers will be there every time you turn around."

"But I'm married to you. Loria Security's most clever operative. Why do we need them?"

Her smile now beamed. "Amos, I appreciate that more than any love words you could have spoken. I *am* good."

He loved the way she soaked up the praise. "You were brilliant in my office. And whatever my employees paid, you were all worth it." Not for the first time, he wondered where the money had come from. "I don't suppose you know how they managed that."

"Not in detail. Jeanette admitted to some fancy manipulation of what she called 'undesignated' funds." Meg sighed gustily. "Unlike me, who is going to have to use my own cash to pay my father back for outbidding Jillian to get you."

He couldn't believe what he was hearing. "Paul made you bid for me out of your own money?"

"Not exactly. He gave me five thousand dollars.

But when I saw how determined Jillian was, I, of course, had to go higher. And by then I was already a little bit in love with you.''

"Why?" He liked the idea, but it surprised him. "You hadn't even met me."

She looked into his eyes, her own reflecting an anticipation that seemed to be accompanied by a trace of fear. "'All for Love' is my favorite song, too. And 'May I have this dance?' happens to be my favorite pickup line."

He put his fork down and dropped his napkin on the table. A man who didn't run with good information didn't deserve to be in business—or in a woman's arms. "May I have this dance?" he asked.

Meg took his hand, and as he led her to the dance floor, he silently blessed her dotty grandmother's fortuitous confusion.

MEG HAD HEARD IT SAID that slow dancing was nothing more than foreplay, and though she'd had very little experience with the latter, she became convinced after only three bluesy tunes in the band's romance retrospective that it was true.

She didn't know if a merging of lives automatically reconfigured anatomy so that a merging of bodies was achieved with startling ease, but she'd never been quite so aware before of how perfectly she fit into Amos's arms.

As a torchy trumpet filled the room with "It Had to Be You," he held her very close, an intimacy that made her breathlessly aware of how malleable her curves were in relationship to the solid planes of his body.

Then "Unforgettable" kept them very close while building the need for a more intimate and prolonged contact.

By the time the band moved on to "As Time Goes By," Meg was wondering if hyperventilation was the usual prelude to lovemaking.

Amos stopped dancing and ran a hand gently up and down her spinal column. He looked a little worried. "Am I going to have to find a paper bag for you to breathe into?" he asked, half-teasing, half-concerned.

She managed a little laugh. "Actually, I was considering a tank of oxygen."

"What's the matter?" he asked, still stroking gently.

"I think," she replied with an embarrassed but smiling glance at him, "it's performance anxiety. Maybe if we just...went upstairs."

He stopped long enough to sign the tab, then led her across the lobby to the elevators.

She knew her brothers would be right behind them, keeping watch from their room across the hall. Even with her body's agitated state of awareness, Meg wondered fleetingly whether or not her father would part company with Jeannette tonight.

Once the elevator doors closed behind them, Amos stayed a small distance from her, as though giving her room to breathe. "I know you can't help what you feel," he said gently, "but performance anxiety is ridiculous. You can throw me across the room, re-member?''

The anxiety she'd tried to suppress all evening was suddenly bubbling up out of control. She concentrated on breathing in and breathing out.

''I know...it's stupid...''

''Well, let's relieve your mind right now,'' he said, ''by eliminating the source of your anxiety.''

She studied him worriedly. ''You're going to leave?''

He laughed. ''No. But we won't make love tonight. We'll just wait until you're comfortable with the idea. It's going to happen—we're too perfect together. So just put it out of your mind. Forget it. We'll watch television or make nuisance phone calls to people we don't like.''

The elevator doors opened on their floor and he handed her the card key to their suite. ''Here,'' he said, ''take this.''

''Why...?'' She began to ask, but was stopped midquestion as he swept her up into his arms.

''Because you'll have to open the door,'' he replied. ''I have my hands full. This isn't our final, official threshold, but this will do for now.''

He walked sideways with her out of the elevator and paused to study her in teasing concern. ''This isn't going to make you pass out or anything, is it?''

She slapped his shoulder. ''It isn't nice to tease someone in the middle of an anxiety attack.''

''The anxiety should be over,'' he said, carrying her to their suite. ''Unlock it for us, will you, please?''

Her left hand holding on to his neck, she inserted the card with her right and was rewarded with the green dot of light. She opened the door.

He walked in with her, catching the door with his shoulder, then closing it with his foot. She held tightly to his neck when he would have put her down in the middle of the living room.

"I have a better idea," she said, praying that her courage would not outdistance the abilities of her body.

"A better idea than what?" he asked.

"Than watching television or making nuisance phone calls."

"Ah. And that would be?"

"That you take me right to the bed and make love to me, only…I hope I'm wrong about not being good at it, but you have to be prepared for that to be…" She felt her throat try to close around a breath. "To be…true."

"I'm sure that it's not," he said. "All it takes is feeling for each other, and we have that."

"I know. But I thought I had it for Daniel."

"Has it occurred to you that Daniel might not have had the right feelings for you?"

That had become clear to her when she thought about the way he'd simply not shown up at the courthouse without telling her, and then faxed her his goodbye. Such behavior was totally callous and unforgivable. Maybe she shouldn't have expected any more from his lovemaking.

"You said he never told you how it was for him," Amos continued, "and that it was all over quicker than you'd expected. That doesn't sound like a man who's taking care of his woman to me."

A small light appeared in the fog of her sexual experience. "You really think so?"

"You want to find out?" he countered.

"Yes," she said. "I do."

He grinned. "You promise to keep breathing?"

She tightened her grip on him and thought she felt the pressure in her chest abate just a little. "Mouth-to-mouth resuscitation would fit in, wouldn't it?"

He laughed and kissed her as he carried her into the bedroom. "It always helps to keep a sense of humor about this. You're going to be fine. Lights on or off?"

She was determined to push aside all her performance concerns, so she didn't want to be worried about what she looked like—not this time anyway. "Is off okay?"

"Sure." He set her down at the foot of the bed and went back to the doorway to flip off the light.

Meg felt a soothing darkness surround her and relaxed another notch. Then Amos was back, his hand falling unerringly on her shoulder.

"That's good," he said. "You didn't jump."

She felt the warmth emanating from him, the energy, and when she put her hand to his chest, his beating heart. She could have sworn the tempo picked up a little when she touched him. At that knowledge, her own heartbeat responded.

"You lead the way," he said, threading his fingers through her hair, "so that I know what you want."

"But how will I know what *you* want?" she asked with what she considered great practicality.

"What I want isn't important tonight."

She leaned into him and wrapped her arms around his waist. "Of course it is. I want us to make love to each other."

He gently wrapped his arms around her and lowered his head to rub his cheek against hers. "Oh, Meg," he said, his voice a little ragged. "It isn't going to take much to give me what I want."

Determinedly she pushed aside her few but fatal memories of her own experiences and thought about how this was done in books and movies. She ran her hands down the front of his polo shirt. "Shall I take this off you?" she asked.

"By all means," he replied, lending her a hand to free it from his slacks.

She pushed the shirt up his chest to his shoulders and stood on tiptoe as he lowered his head to allow her to pull it off.

"The belt?"

"Sure."

She unbuckled it easily, then unfastened the button at his waistband. She was about to put her fingertips to his zipper, her cheeks warming, then—practically—remembered his shoes.

Placing her hands on his arms, she turned him around so that they switched places, then urged him down onto the foot of the bed.

"Shoes next," she said, sweeping her hands to his knees and lifting his lower leg. As she untied his shoelace, she felt him lean back, probably propping himself on his elbows.

"I never thought having your shoes removed could be seductive," he said, his voice rich and deep in the darkness. "But it is."

When she had removed his shoe and sock, he rested his foot in her hand.

"Are you ticklish?" she asked, running a fingernail lightly up the sole of his foot.

"Yes…" He expelled a strained breath. "But not there. That feels…well, here's the other foot."

When it too was bare, she ran a finger down it, eliciting the same whispered groan from him. It made her bold enough to say, "Slacks next."

"Good idea," he agreed, and she heard the snick of a zipper. "Any time you're ready."

Grasping the pant legs, she tugged. His slacks came off with ease.

"Must be nice," she teased, "not to have hips that make that difficult."

"Hips look good on a woman," he said, a smile in his voice. There was a moment's pause, then he asked gently, "Want me to do the rest?"

"No," she said, and leaned over him, determined to be as eager to do for him as he was for her. She touched him and felt his thighs again, warm, muscular, lean. Before she could reconsider, she ran her fingers up to the waistband of his briefs, slipped her fingers beneath and edged them down.

"Still breathing?" he asked, though he sounded as though he were the one having difficulty.

"Just," she said, her heart skipping out of control. "But I don't think it's fear anymore."

"Told you. Now what?"

AMOS SUPPRESSED the impulse to dispense with her dress and everything else she wore, reminding himself that he'd put her in charge. She was doing beautifully, but she might be afraid to let him undress her.

Then her voice came to him through the darkness. "I have my back to you. This has a zipper."

He stood and found her shoulders, then the zipper pull right between them. He eased it down, then slid the dress off her shoulders, moving slowly so as not to alarm her. Catching her elbow, he helped her step out of the dress.

He saw a pale white glow in the darkness. "Slip?"

"Mmm," she replied, turning to face him.

His heartbeat beginning to distract him, he reached for the spot where the glow disappeared in the darkness, found handfuls of lace and lifted them up. She raised her arms as he pulled the silky garment off.

"Still okay?" he asked. He saw bands of ivory on an alabaster form—her bra and panties.

"Yeah," she said.

"Good. Because I'm about to croak from desire. I'm also changing my mind about black lace. I wouldn't be able to see that in the dark." He was about to ask her if she wanted to remove the last two items herself when he saw her turn, offering him her back again.

With trembling fingers, he found two small hooks and undid them. To his complete surprise, she leaned back against him, and he raised his hands to touch her. Afraid that wasn't what she'd intended, he was about to lower them again when she caught his hands and placed them over her breasts.

The tips of her nipples beaded against his palm as he leaned down to kiss her throat. He whispered her name and she arched her head back to allow him access, then turned her entire body in his arms.

"You're in charge now," she said, her voice husky as she wrapped her arms around his neck. "I feel so...wonderful."

He braced an arm under her bottom and lifted her onto his hip. "Just wait," he promised, walking around the bed with her. He set her on her feet, then yanked the bedspread back and pushed her gently onto the bed. Holding on to his arms, she brought him down with her.

He kissed her throat and swept a hand down her silk-clad stomach. "These have to come off, you know," he teased.

"I bought them with you in mind," she said, "so treat them with respect."

"The way I feel right now," he said, sitting up to dispense with them, "we could have them bronzed."

MEG DIDN'T FEEL AT ALL like herself. She felt more at home in her body than she ever had before.

She was going to be okay, she thought happily. Even if it hurt, she would be all right, though she had it on Jamie's authority that it didn't have to.

At the thought, she tensed just a little.

But Amos seemed in no hurry. He stroked her hair

back and kissed her. "Is this where the trouble usually starts?" he asked softly.

"Yes." She tightened her grip on his neck. "But at least you're not yelling directions at me."

He raised his head to look down at her. "Directions?"

"About what to do."

He swore. "That must have been a lot of fun."

"To Daniel's credit, the directions were supposed to ease the discomfort."

"It's not supposed to be uncomfortable."

"Well, maybe I'm just dif—"

"You're not different." He pulled her up and settled her in the crook of his arm, leaning his upper body over her. "Just relax and trust me that this will be something you'll want to do again."

"It doesn't matter, Amos. I'll be fi—"

She stopped abruptly when his fingers dipped between her thighs, exploring in caressing circles. She felt a strange languor start to come over her, but when he dipped a fingertip tentatively inside her, her body tightened instinctively.

"Easy," Amos whispered, leaning down to touch a kiss to the tip of one breast, then the other. "And that's not a direction, it's a recommendation."

"But..." she said, feeling a tug inside her abdomen that made her wonder if she was going to pass out on him after all. "I...don't think I have..."

"Have what?"

"*You know*..." She was beginning to feel an unusual tension building within her as his fingers continued their circular motion. "Or maybe it doesn't work."

"Doesn't...?"

She didn't hear the rest of his question because she suddenly discovered that she was wrong.

Very wrong.

She heard Big Ben ring in London. Planets collided. Somewhere very near, a high, perfect note was sounded that found its echo in her and played on and on and on. It stunned her with its purity, shook her with its power, changed her forever with its beauty.

When it was over, she couldn't think, couldn't speak. Amos leaned over her and kissed her lips. "Repeat after me," he said. "I will never doubt Amos again."

It was all she could do not to shout, "It wasn't me! It never was me!"

She pushed him onto his back and leaned over him. "I want to do that for you."

He laughed softly. "I'm all yours."

Hesitantly she placed a hand on his stomach, then immediately withdrew it. "If you don't like it, you have to say."

"Oh, Meg..." He took her hand and put it back on him. "There isn't a fraction of a chance that I'm not going to like it."

Though she trusted Amos, she couldn't imagine being able to do for him what he'd done for her.

Until she did.

And then he swept a leg over her, braced his forearms on either side of her and entered her with a smooth and easy movement. She remembered her earlier thought about love making bodies fit, and realized what a miracle it was to feel this way, as though life were a puzzle, and they were the last two missing pieces.

The pleasure came over her again in waves, and as one they rolled over until she was uppermost and aware of an even more exquisite sensation.

As she leaned down to kiss his shoulders, his pecs, his abdomen, he caressed her and drove her to pleasure a delicious third time.

When at last she collapsed on top of him, he enveloped her in his embrace, kissing her temple and her cheek. "I hate to say I told you so again," he whispered, nipping at her earlobe, "but I told you so."

CHAPTER TWELVE

AMOS WAS SO BUSY writing up sales at the show on Sunday that Meg was on her own, wandering around the hall. The euphoria of their lovemaking was still with her, and she felt a little as though she were traveling on a cushion of air. It hadn't been her fault! A night in Amos's arms had taught her that she *was* a sexual woman, equipped to accept pleasure and provide it with equal fervor. The relief she felt was indescribable.

When she stopped to read the menu at a refreshment stand, a young male voice from beside her asked, "Buy you a pop?"

Meg turned to find Kyle standing next to her, a five-dollar bill in his hand. "Amos is busy, but he saw you walking this way and sent me to buy you something to drink."

"Can you stay and join me?"

He nodded. "I'd like to talk to you. Large, medium or small?"

"Medium, please."

"Do you want anything with it?"

"Want to split a brownie?"

He checked the menu, calculated the cost, then nodded.

Meg found a table and he joined her in a moment,

handing her the brownie and a coffee stir stick with which to cut it in half.

"No knives," he said with a grin. "I guess they don't trust toy people with sharp instruments."

Meg laughed and wielded the stick.

"What did you want to talk to me about?" she asked, handing him half the brownie on one of the napkins he'd brought.

"Your dad," he said, taking a large bite of the sweet. He chewed and swallowed and took a long gulp of cola. "He's cool for an old guy. I mean, not *cool* like...you know, he dresses like he works in a bank, and he doesn't like rock, but he's cool. He comes over when he says he's going to, he brings my mom flowers, and he says he wants to take me to the coin and stamp show."

"He has very impressive collections," Meg said. "You like coins and stamps?"

Kyle shook his head honestly. "No, but I like it that he wants to take me. My dad never wanted to take me anywhere."

"Well. My father's very good at being a dad, because when I was growing up, my mom had died and he had to be everything to my brothers and me."

Kyle nodded. He played with the straw in his cola, putting a finger over the top, then raising the straw and lifting his finger to watch the pop stream back into the cup. "So you think there's a chance I'm going to like...be your stepbrother?"

Meg looked up at Amos's booth and saw Jeannette writing orders while Meg's father demonstrated a space ship to an interested shopper, clearly trying to help.

"We might be rushing things...but it's entirely possible," Meg replied. "I'd really like that."

Kyle grinned. "And you could maybe teach me that martial arts stuff."

"I could do that, anyway."

"*That* would be cool."

The crowd of people lined up at the Pike's Pickled Pepper booth was growing. Meg downed the last bite of her brownie and gestured Kyle to follow her. "I think we'd better see if we can help. You know all about the toys. You can talk them up while I see what I can do."

WHILE MEG AND HER brothers began to disassemble the booth that afternoon, Amos looked quickly through the sales orders and let out a low whistle.

Jeannette glanced over his shoulder. "Yeah, I know," she said. "We're going to have to put on another shift or something. Do you think we can meet all those orders?"

Amos nodded, feeling the thrill of having conceived, designed and produced something that a boy like Kyle had found "really cool" and experienced buyers believed would be the Christmas season's hottest toy.

And even more than the promised financial success of the space station, he took great satisfaction in the fact that the toy would provide so much fun for so many kids. That meant everything to him.

"I suspected it would be a hit," he said, "so the plant's ready. These orders will allow raises and bonuses, so if we have to push a little harder, I don't think the employees will mind."

Jeannette reached up to kiss his cheek. "You're okay, Pike."

"Hey!" Paul complained, boxing toys. "You're a married man and Jeannette has a date with me tonight."

"You have a date with all of us," Brian said. He stood on a ladder and removed a one-by-four that formed the top of the booth, handing it down to Ben. "You said you were taking everybody to dinner to celebrate the end of the case."

"The end?" Jeannette asked. "We got the space station safely to the show, but..."

Paul nodded. "Jillian put her business and her house up for sale. The real estate agent confirmed it for me."

She closed her eyes. "I can't believe it. Free at last."

Once everything was loaded onto a hand truck to take out to the van in the parking lot, Amos took a look around to make sure he hadn't forgotten anything.

Then he suddenly realized something important was missing. "Where's Meg?" he asked.

Jeannette pointed toward the far side of the hall. "Ladies' room."

"Ah. Where are we having dinner?" he asked Paul.

"The Gold Pagoda in Chinatown?"

"Sounds good. Go on ahead. Meg and I'll meet you there."

Paul hesitated doubtfully as his sons rolled the hand truck toward the door.

Amos slapped him on the shoulder. "Hey. You can break the habit of watching out for me. And anyway,

I'll have Meg with me. It's time you gave her credit for how good she is at what she does.''

"I know." Paul picked up his jacket. "I've tried to explain to her that I don't ever question her skill. It's just a possessive father thing. Her mother and I were so thrilled to have a girl after three boys. I think even *they* were glad to have her. She'll always be my baby and their little sister, no matter how expert an operative she is. See you at the restaurant.''

Amos headed in the direction of the rest rooms to wash his hands, which were a peculiar shade of blue from all the sales orders he'd written.

Only two other people remained in the hall, and he waved at them as they headed toward the doors.

"Meg!" he shouted into the entrance of the ladies' room. A large bank of phones separated it from the hall, but it was open at both sides. "I'm going to wash my hands. We're meeting your dad at the Gold Pagoda, so just wait for me by our stuff where the booth was.''

"Okay!" she shouted back.

Amos washed his hands, ran a comb through his hair and decided that he probably looked respectable enough to go to dinner. The Pike's Polar Bear shirt was a little the worse for wear, but he'd throw his jacket on over it and no one would notice.

He left the men's room, expecting Meg to be standing by their things, but she wasn't there. He leaned against the wall and waited a few minutes. When she still didn't emerge, he went to the doorway of the ladies' room and called her name again.

There was no answer. He turned to do another perusal of the hall and found it completely empty.

The hair along the back of his neck rose without

warning, and a sense of foreboding seeped into every little corner of his being. He remembered Jillian's smile that afternoon, and knew he'd trusted it only because he'd been so complacent in his happiness with Meg.

He walked into the ladies' room. "Meg!" he shouted again.

Something moved in the corner, and he turned his head to see Jillian pushing Meg in front of her. She had a fistful of Meg's hair and held a gun to her throat.

Terror flared in his gut but lasted only an instant. Then anger roared to life, harsh and lethal. He noticed absently that his brain remained remarkably clear.

"You couldn't beat me at business," he observed calmly as Jillian cocked a bullet into the chamber, and Meg closed her eyes, helpless, "so you're out to destroy my personal life."

"I've always loved your nimble brain, darling," Jillian said. "You didn't really think I'd be able to settle down with a bunch of cows, did you?"

"I hoped so," he said, frantically trying to come up with a plan. So far he had nothing. "This way, you're going to end up in jail with your 'cattle buyers.' And I'm still going to have everything."

Jillian tugged harder on Meg's hair. "Are you blind, darling? I have a gun to your little wife's throat."

"I see that. But you don't really think I'm going to let you hurt her."

"I don't see how you can stop me. So even though you think you have everything, Amos, my love, you don't. You *could* have had it with me, but you were so stingy."

"You cheated, Jill."

She rolled her eyes. "Cheated," she repeated scornfully. "Business is tricky, Amos, if you want to stay on top. I was just doing a little creative research. It seemed foolish to research that technology in a lab when you'd already figured it out."

"That isn't business, Jillian, it's stealing."

Jillian just shook her head at him. "We could have ruled the toy business, you and I."

He shook his head. "Meg and I are going to do that."

"Meg is going to be dead!" Jillian roared in a sudden rage.

Amos knew this was not going to be one of those situations where he advanced toward her calmly with his hand held out, saying, "Give me the gun." This was a ruthless woman deranged by her losses and anxious to make someone pay for them.

He held his arms out to show his helplessness. "But I'm the one who destroyed you. Why shoot her?"

"Because that will destroy *you!*" she said with wild-eyed delight. "And that would be more satisfying to me than killing you."

Taking the only chance he had, even though it was a long shot, Amos took a step toward her, pretending to glance behind her with a quick shake of his head.

She started to look back, then grinned and tightened her grip on Meg. "I know there's no one behind me," she said. "There was no one in here when I came in, and no one's gotten past me."

"Are you forgetting the back door?"

"There is no back door."

"Are you sure?"

"I'm sure," she said, but she wasn't. Her eyes scanned the room, and her movements became agitated and uncertain. She cocked the pistol.

Amos made an instant decision. He glanced over her head again and waited until she half turned to be sure there was no one there. In that split second he leaped toward her, figuring that with the barrel of the gun angled as she turned, he would be hit if it went off, and not Meg.

The report was loud and instant as the three of them landed in a heap on the tiled floor. But he felt no pain.

Oh, God, no! He scrambled to his knees, sure the bullet must have struck Meg. But she was reaching for him, stunned but unhurt.

He held her to him with one arm, then reached around her to take the gun from Jillian's slack hand. On the bottom of the pile, Jillian lay knocked unconscious by the fall. A towel dispenser fell to the floor with a clatter, a bullet hole in its white metal housing.

Then Paul and Brian appeared, stopping just inside the room at the sight of the three of them.

Amos explained briefly what happened while Brian called the police.

"Instinct brought me back," Paul said, helping Amos pull Meg to her feet. "I wish it had been quicker. I knew Jillian was ruthless, but I didn't realize she'd gone crazy on us."

"Nobody can second-guess everything." Amos looked at Meg. "You okay, Meg?" She stood quietly in the circle of his arm, but there was a pleat between her eyebrows he didn't understand. She looked almost as though *she* didn't understand what had happened.

He put a hand to her head, feeling for bumps. "Did you get hurt when we fell?"

"No," she replied, her attention only half on him. "I'm fine."

"She get the drop on you?" Paul asked.

She looked up then, her complete attention focused on her father, and said with a nod, "Yeah. She did."

"That happens, you know," Paul said.

She tucked her disheveled hair behind her ear. "Not to me."

"It's happened to me. You consider yourself better at this than I am?"

Though she seemed more aware, her expression remained grim. "It's not a matter of who's better."

"That's right," her father said, "it isn't. So let it go."

FOR THE THIRD TIME in the brief nine days Meg and Amos had known each other, they spent hours with the police. When they were finished, Jillian Chambers was booked for assault with a deadly weapon and held for psychiatric evaluation, and Loria Security's assignment to protect Amos Pike was officially closed.

"I wish you'd talk about what happened," Amos said to Meg as they rode the elevator up to their suite in the Fulton Towers Hotel. "I know that had to be terrifying. It's all right for you to admit that, you know."

Meg stood in the opposite corner from him, lost within herself. She knew Amos was upset by the emotional distance she'd kept since he had picked her up off the ladies' room floor. But she didn't know how to explain what was going on inside her.

She didn't know who she was anymore. Though her family's protectiveness had long been a sore spot with her, she'd prided herself on the knowledge that she was competent and intelligent, and when it came to their work, she was as good as any of her brothers.

She'd worried about her sexual self, but last night Amos had put all those fears to rest. For the first time in her adult life, she felt whole.

But that victory had been destroyed when she'd stared at herself in the rest room mirror that stretched above the sinks in the convention hall's ladies' room. She'd been reliving the night before, thinking about how much in love she was, how lucky she'd been that Grandma Rooney had gotten Daniel and Amos confused.

Then, suddenly, there'd been another face in the mirror, and Jillian Chambers was pointing a gun to her ear.

At first she'd been shocked that she'd allowed that to happen—while looking in a mirror! It wasn't easy for someone to sneak up behind you when you could see everything reflected in the mirror.

She'd always been so careful, so alert, so attuned to her surroundings. But in this case she'd wasted precious time wondering what had happened.

Then Amos had walked in, and the sight of his face—pale but calm—had made her forget everything she'd ever known about self-defense. Her brain had been so cluttered with love and fear for him, fear of how she would go on if she lost him, that she literally couldn't do her job.

Assessing the situation later, she realized she'd had several options that would have been risky but possible. But at the time, it hadn't occurred to her to try anything. Years of training and experience had been worth absolutely nothing when she faced the possibility of losing what she and Amos had found together.

He caught her arm and drew her with him as the elevator doors opened, and she waited beside him while he unlocked their suite.

"I was so scared," she admitted, "that I couldn't do my job."

He frowned at her as he held the door open for her to pass through. "Someone was holding a loaded gun to your throat." He locked the door, tossed the key on a fussy little credenza, then took her with him to a brocade settee. He sat down and pulled her down beside him.

"You still think of me as a job?" he asked, his voice reflecting surprise and amusement.

"Protecting you was my job," she said, ignoring his attempt to charm her. "And I didn't do it."

"Meg." He caught her hands and tugged on her so she was forced to look at him. "That's ridiculous. You were helpless."

"She sneaked up on me in a mirror!" she shouted, some emotional knot inside her snapping. "Because I was thinking about you! Then when I saw you walk in...I panicked!"

"You didn't panic. You never made a sound. You just waited for—"

"No! I wasn't waiting for anything! I was frozen! Paralyzed! Scared!"

He drew a breath, clearly not understanding why he wasn't getting through to her. "You had a gun to your throat."

"But I was trained to know what to do under even

the worst circumstances! And I couldn't even think! I didn't have one idea! If you hadn't shown up, she'd have killed me and then you, and we never would've had four kids to send to Harvard!''

HE WAS JUST BEGINNING to understand what was going on here—and it was both good and bad. Their relationship had become so important to her that the possibility of losing it had shocked her into forgetting the skills she knew as well as her own name.

But something even worse than that seemed to be happening. He could feel her pulling away from him. Was she thinking that if loving him meant losing her edge as a bodyguard, she had to choose between him or her work?

He searched his mind for a reasonable argument. "You reacted like someone in love," he said. "I don't mind knowing that."

"You didn't forget to be brave," she countered. "I saw the love and fear in your eyes, but you took a chance and came right at the bullet!"

"Because you're everything to me. I did what was instinctive, I didn't have to remember training."

She stood and paced across the room, stopping to study the ornate gilt-trimmed clock. "I just keep wondering if *my* instinct was waiting for my brothers to rescue me."

He followed her, stopping several feet from her when her eyes insisted that he keep his distance. He leaned against the back of a brocade chair. "Meg, it had nothing to do with that. You weren't afraid for yourself, you were afraid of losing *us*. I guess that's the price of loving someone. Now we have something to lose."

She put a hand to her forehead. "I can't face the fact that I'm going to be a coward for the rest of my life."

When she went to the bedroom, he followed again, stopping in the doorway. She pulled her small weekend bag out of the closet and put it on the bed.

If she wanted to experience real cowardice, he thought, she should feel what he felt at this moment. "What are you doing?" he made himself ask calmly.

"I think I should go home for a while," she said, going to the closet to snatch the few things she'd hung up for their two-day stay.

"How is that going to help?"

"I don't know. But if I stay here with you..." She shook her head and carelessly dropped the things into her bag. "My feelings for you seem to grow exponentially. I should be completely worthless in another four or five days."

He walked into the room, ignoring her keep-your-distance stare. This was almost worse than the ladies' room incident. He shifted his weight. "All that's happened, Meg," he said, "is that for once, you didn't react like the security machine you've trained yourself to be to compete with your brothers. Last night you discovered you're not a machine, you're a woman. That's good, not bad."

"It made me lose control!" she shouted at him, going to the dresser to grab a small bag from the top of it.

"Love isn't about control or power, it's about surrender. I suppose that's hard for a security specialist to accept, but there you are. Maybe you're going to have to consider a career change."

She tossed the bag at her case, then ripped a drawer

open and pulled a small pile of silky things out of it. "Maybe I have to consider an annulment."

Her words felt like a blunt trowel right to the heart. He straightened, desperate to reach her. "If our marriage comes second to your need for power over every situation," he said, "then maybe you should."

"We got married," she reminded him, "so that my grandmother would give Becky the funding for her program."

He met her eyes, letting her see what he knew to be true. "That was the excuse you used. I didn't realize it then, but that was probably because it gave you power over the situation. But I know that you jumped at my suggestion because you loved me. You love me now. You'll always love me, and the fact that you choose to walk away rather than surrender to that isn't going to change it or even diminish it. What about the four kids we were going to send to Harvard?"

That did it. She looked at him as though he'd just slapped her, her eyes huge and hurt, then stormed into the bathroom and slammed the door.

He didn't know if he was prompted by the need to keep her there, or simply by exasperation, but he considered calling the front desk for bricks and mortar.

CHAPTER THIRTEEN

AMOS WENT DOWN to the lounge for a drink. He decided against joining the lively group at the bar and found an elegantly upholstered bench in a dark and quiet corner. He downed half his gin and tonic before letting himself think about Meg and what he was going to do about her.

It was ironic, he thought, that he could solve any design problem presented to him on the drawing board, but given a flesh-and-blood woman and the need to find a way to fit her life to his, he was at a loss.

A small pain burned hot right in the middle of his chest. He'd really enjoyed thinking about those four kids they were going to send to Harvard. He couldn't imagine that dream would dissolve because Meg couldn't accept her own vulnerabilities and limitations.

He finished his drink and ordered a ginger ale. There had to be a solution here. He just had to stop thinking in a linear way.

"Amos?"

A small, frail voice jolted him out of his thoughts and had him halfway to his feet before he realized it belonged to Jeannette and not Meg. He swallowed disappointment and tried to force a smile—then realized with a second look at Jeannette's face that she didn't appear at all in the mood for cheer, forced or otherwise.

He caught her arm and pulled her down beside him on the bench. She still wore the dark slacks and company shirt she'd worn to the show, but the cheerful glow she'd had all day had been replaced by a profound sadness.

She put her satchel purse on the floor beside her and clasped her hands between her knees, as though shriveling in upon herself to avoid something unpleasant.

"What happened?" he asked. There'd be time to concentrate on his problems later.

"I wouldn't have bothered you," she said with a questioning glance at him. "But I saw you sitting here, all alone."

"Yeah." He ignored that observation. "What's wrong?"

When she opened her mouth to try to speak, her face crumpled. She put a hand up to cover it. "I'm sorry." Her apology was high and squeaky.

He raised his hand for the cocktail waitress. Since Jeannette had now dissolved into noisy tears, he ordered her a glass of chardonnay, remembering that she ordered it for herself whenever they lunched with customers.

He patted her back, wondering what had happened to reduce this tower-of-strength woman to a puddle of tears.

"Is it Kyle?" he asked.

She shook her head, still sobbing. "No. He's... great."

"Money? Because if that's a problem, I'm sure there's something we can..."

She gave him a grateful look over a cocktail napkin held to her mouth, then shook her head adamantly.

"You're not sick?"

Another negative. She sat up straighter, took a deep sip of her wine and seemed to be make a desperate effort to pull herself together. "It's Paul!" The words came out like a broken groan.

"What happened to Paul?" he asked anxiously. It had been a long few hours at the police station and he wasn't a young man.

She took his napkin, too, and dabbed at her eyes. "Nothing. Except that I think I've scared him to death."

He waited for her to explain.

"I told him I loved him," she said calmly, then started to cry all over again. "He called the Golden Pagoda from the police station," she said, once she had regained her control, "because Ben and Father Frank and I had already left for the restaurant when you had the confrontation with Jillian." She paused long enough to say, "I'm so glad you're all right. And that Meg wasn't hurt."

He nodded and handed her her wine. "Thanks. Drink up. I still don't understand the problem."

She took two deep gulps and held the glass in her lap. "We'd all been eating hors d'oeuvres, waiting for you guys, wondering where you were. Then when we heard what happened, we were in no mood to stay, so Father Frank said we should go back to the hotel suite with them and wait for all of you to return. Ben and Frank took Kyle down to the arcade to play games and I was alone in the suite when Paul finally walked in. I..." She paused to finish the wine, then placed the empty glass on the table and stared at it, as though it were significant. "I was so glad to see him. It had been such a wonderful day—all of us working together—and I'd been thinking how... important he'd become to me in such a short time. I threw my arms around him and..." Her eyes expressed her own surprise. "It just sort of came out. 'I love you.' Just like that. 'I love you.' After you've been hurt the way I was with Kyle's father, you become very careful to hold those words in, to keep them to yourself on the chance you'll be hurt again. But..." She sighed unhappily. "They just came out of their own accord—I couldn't help it."

"But that isn't bad, is it?" he asked. "I've been watching you two, and there is something special going on."

A tear slid down her cheek. "I thought so, too. But...you know...he's raised his children, he has a business that leaves him time to relax and—" She waved a hand to indicate whatever it was he might do in his leisure time. "Why would he need anything to complicate his life?"

That didn't sound like the Paul Meg had talked about all week, the man he'd come to know in two brief days.

"What did he say?" Amos asked.

"I can't remember exactly," she said, calm now. She took his half-empty glass. "May I have this?"

"Sure."

She downed it in one swallow, then grimaced. "It's ginger ale!" she complained.

He took the glass from her. "You'd like straight whiskey, maybe? You were telling me what he said."

She sighed with a deep-down misery. "It amounted to 'thanks, but no thanks.'"

"Are you sure? What were his words?"

She fixed him with a condemning look. "Trust me to know a rejection when I hear one, Amos. What are you doing down here, anyway? This is the night after your wedding night. It should still be going on."

He raised his hand to order two cups of coffee. "Yeah, well, things aren't always the way they should be, are they?"

Jeannette leaned against the back of the bench and sighed dejectedly. "We're going to die at our desks, aren't we? Two people who just can't find someone to love them. So, we'll have nothing but our work." She elbowed him in the ribs, grim humor flickering in her eyes. "I, at least, might have grandchildren."

Yeah, Amos thought. All he'd have was the dream of four smart little kids who could have gone to Harvard.

MEG HEARD AMOS LEAVE the suite and came out of the bathroom to finish her packing. If she was lucky, she could be gone before he returned.

That was such a cowardly thought, it only served to confirm what she already knew. Love had turned her into a worthless human being.

She snapped her bag closed, spotted the Pike's polar bear on her pillow, and decided with the only glimpse of spine she'd shown since the Jillian episode to leave it there and walk away.

As she walked toward the bedroom door, an unbidden memory came to her of Amos at the auction, looking wonderfully sexy in his tux as he tossed the bear at the crowd of eager women.

She ran back to the bed, snatched up the bear, and held it to her face as she burst into tears.

A loud banging on the door brought her out of her self-indulgence and made her drop the bear back on the bed.

They'd all been stupid to think their crazy scheme would work, she thought as she walked across the carpet. Actually, that wasn't accurate. Jeannette had been desperate enough to think it would, and her father's job had been to see to his client's wishes. She, Margaret Guinevere Loria, had been stupid to think she could turn a deception like that into a marriage.

"Dad?" Her father stood in the open doorway, then marched past her into the room, hands in his pockets, a deep pucker of worry just above the bridge of his nose.

He paced across the room to the window, looked out, then came back again. He stopped in front of the settee and glanced around. "Where's Amos?" he asked.

"Uh...not sure," she replied, bracing herself for some sort of lecture on the foolishness of misplacing a husband.

But he didn't seem concerned about her problems at the moment. He fell onto the settee and asked plaintively, "How in the hell did I get to be so old, anyway?"

She stared at him, wondering at his uncharacteristic and inconveniently timed self-reflection. She didn't have time for this. She had to be gone before Amos got back.

But she couldn't remember an instance in her life when her father hadn't had time for her. She sat beside him on the settee.

"Dad, what are you talking about?" she asked.

"Me!" he said, pointing a thumb at himself. "Old!

Sixty-three in September. What am I supposed to do with a woman who tells me she loves me?''

Ah. ''Jeannette told you she loved you?''

''Yeah.'' He leaned against the hard back of the little sofa and dropped his head onto the pointed carvings of the woodwork.

Meg flinched but he didn't seem to notice. He simply stared at the ceiling.

''What could I give a forty-one-year-old woman and a twelve-year-old boy?'' he asked. ''I mean, I hoped I could offer them something. I wanted to. But when she flew into my arms and told me she loved me, I thought, 'Get real, Loria! What do you think you're doing here? She needs a...a younger, more virile man. And the kid should have a father who understands about rock music, and Rollerblades and earrings.''

''He'd have Grandma Rooney for that,'' Meg said with a laugh.

Her father didn't find it funny.

She sobered instantly. ''Sorry. Look.'' She turned sideways to get his full attention. ''Are you telling me that Jeannette declared her love for you and you...didn't respond?''

''I...'' He put a hand to his forehead. ''I don't remember it clearly. I was kind of in shock, you know. I mean, I knew I loved her, but I had no idea she felt the same. So I said something about, uh, being too old for her and set in my ways and used to my quiet and my leisure and...''

''Dad!''

He flinched and folded his arms. ''Well, it's true,'' he said defensively. ''I'm twenty-one years older than she is. Even if I could...you know...'' He cast her an embarrassed glance that she understood instantly because she'd been there herself last night. "Maybe I'd make her happy this year, and maybe next year, but what about the year after that, and however long we'd have together?"

Meg put a hand to his shoulder. She'd never seen him this defenseless. "Daddy, sex isn't everything."

He gave her a scolding glance. She presumed it was for having used the word. "No, it isn't, but it's damned important. And the younger you are, the more important it is."

"Well, you're in good health," she pointed out reasonably. "How do you know it would be a problem?"

"Like I said, it might not be a problem now, but what about later?"

"So, you'd pass on what the two of you could have today because of what might happen later?"

He leaned forward, elbows on his knees, and put his face in his hands. "You don't understand."

"Sure I do." She placed an arm around his shoulders. "You're scared. You've had this wonderful little world where you didn't really have to live your own life, all you had to do was oversee the boys' and mine. But this would change all that. You'd actually have to live for yourself."

He dropped his hands and glowered at her. "It isn't nice to dress down your father."

She squeezed his shoulder. "I'm just trying to make you take a second look at this."

"But what about Kyle?" he asked worriedly. "You heard the kid talk about what he's been through. His father didn't want to do things with him. What happens when my arthritis flares up and I can't do whatever he wants to do? Will he think it's because I don't care?''

''Of course not. Because in your minute-to-minute, day-to-day relationship with him, I'm sure you'll be the caring and attentive father you were to Brian and Frank and Ben and me.'' She caught his hands. ''Dad. Don't borrow trouble.''

''I can't help it,'' he admitted. ''I never thought I could have all this again. I'm scared.''

She patted his back. ''Of course you are. Love takes over everything and turns you into someone you don't even recognize.''

He met her eyes. ''Did it do that to you? You seem softer, yet somehow more sure of yourself than the young woman I used to know.''

She had to laugh at that. ''I feel less sure of everything.''

For the first time since her father had walked in the door, he really looked into her eyes. ''Why? What's changed?''

''Nothing much. Anyway, we're talking about you,'' she said, unwilling to complicate his own struggle by adding to it with hers. ''Where's Jeannette now?''

He frowned. ''I'm not sure. Frank and Ben are off with Kyle somewhere, so I don't imagine she's left the hotel.''

She got to her feet and went to call the desk. ''Maybe they've seen her.''

''Yes, Mrs. Pike,'' the desk clerk said, clearly pleased to have an answer for her. ''I saw her in the lounge with Mr. Pike.''

Amos. Amos was in the lounge.

''Thank you,'' she said, and hung up. ''She's in

the lounge with Amos, Dad." She caught her father's arm and led him to the door. "Tell her what's in your heart, and don't be afraid to admit that you're a little scared. She probably is, too."

Paul kept hold of her arm as he moved toward the elevator. "Meg, I'm not sure I know how to do this," he said, the fear coming back to life in his eyes. "What if she's decided I'm not worth it after all? She left in tears just twenty minutes ago."

"Dad..."

"How do I reassure her that she can trust me when I just showed her what a chicken I really am?"

"Daddy..."

"She threw her arms around me and I started talking about how I might collect early social security!"

The elevator doors parted and Ben, Frank and Kyle stepped off.

"Hey, Dad. Meg," Ben said. He pointed to Kyle, who held a giant plush chartreuse monkey. "Look at what he won on the rifle game. I'm telling you, the kid's a natural to join Loria Security when he grows up."

Kyle beamed. "Hi, Paul. Where's Mom?"

"Uh..." Paul reached a hand out to stop the elevator doors from closing. "We're just going to find her."

"Well, bring her back," Frank said. "We're going to order up some onion rings and maybe a gourmet pizza. We never did get to celebrate the end of the case."

Meg tried to free herself from her father's fingers. If she hurried, she could still get away before Amos came back upstairs.

But he had a death grip on her. "Meggie, come down with me in the elevator," he pleaded.

"No, Dad, I..."

"But you just did that thing with Amos while you were in the cabin—you know, finding out what men and women want from each other. You can coach me on the way down. Please? I don't want to blow this."

Ben and Kyle were already heading toward their suite, but Meg turned a look of supplication on Frank. He pushed her onto the elevator with their father and stepped in after them.

"What's going on with you two?" he asked. Both hands in his pockets, he studied one, then the other. "You look as though I should perform the last rites."

"I'm a coward, okay?" Paul admitted. He explained about Jeannette's declaration and her running off in tears. "I came to Meg for advice, but she doesn't want to go this last mile with me. What's the matter with you, anyway?"

"God!" she exclaimed in exasperation, then looked up at Frank in apology. "I'm sorry. I know you don't like it when we do that."

He nodded. "We'll presume that was supplication and not taking His name in vain. What *is* the matter with you?"

The elevator stopped on the fifth floor, but whoever had called it had apparently given up and taken the stairs.

"I've got my own chicken thing going, if you must know. You weren't there, but Jillian got the drop on me in the ladies' room while I was looking in the mirror! I deserve to be drummed out of the bodyguard business!"

"Are you *still* on that?" Paul demanded. "I know

you've always had to be better than any of us just to prove yourself, and you're very good, but none of us is perfect. I don't understand why it's so hard for you to come to terms with that.''

"Amos was in danger!'' she exclaimed, unable to understand why *he* couldn't understand, "and all I could think about was how much I loved him and all the things we were going to do together and the four kids that were going to go to Harvard, and she got the drop on me! And then, when he walked in, instead of my professionalism coming into play to help me save him, all I could think about was, what if I lose him? What if there's no us after all?''

Her question rang in the silence of the elevator, her father staring at her in concern, her brother frowning in concentration.

She looked up at the numbers and saw the elevator pass the second floor and descend toward the lobby. In another minute the doors would open. What if Jeannette had left and Amos was waiting for an elevator to take him back upstairs and she had to ride up with him and remember everything they would never have together?

The elevator stopped, but Frank stabbed an index finger onto the close button.

"Listen to me, both of you,'' he said. "I know I promised when I entered the priesthood that I'd never preach to you, but the moment seems to call for it. At least it'll be brief. Are you listening?''

"Yes,'' Meg said.

Paul sighed. "We're pretty much a captive audience, Frank.''

"All right. It's very simple.'' Frank pointed to

Meg. "You think that loving Amos has turned you into a coward."

"It has."

"No, it hasn't. Because loving is the bravest thing you will ever do in your entire life. It's so big that it diminishes the importance of everything else. You weren't alert because your heart was filled with love. Your need to keep it alive was more important than the need to keep your body alive, that's why you couldn't react. Love doesn't make you a coward, Meg, it makes you a giant."

Love was the bravest thing she would ever do. The words played over again in her mind and finally clicked into place as knowledge.

He turned to Paul. "And you. I remember how much Mom loved you, and I know how much we love you, so don't ever sell yourself short as a potential husband and father for another family, I don't care how old you get to be. You have more guts than any man I know. You can do this."

He dropped his hand from the button. "Now, get off this elevator. I have a party to plan."

The doors parted, a laughing group swarmed on and Meg and Paul fought their way off. Then they looked at each other as they stood alone at the end of the lobby.

"Tell her on second thought you decided you…" Meg stopped when she realized she didn't have her father's attention. He was looking beyond her to the edge of the lobby where the lounge was closed off by ornate stained-glass windows. Jeannette had just walked out of it and was heading toward them, head down, her usual woman-with-a-mission demeanor compromised by a slump to her shoulders and a dispirited air to her step.

She looked up and saw them and stopped abruptly.

"Oh, God," her father said under his breath.

Meg gave him a supportive pat on the back. "Remember. It's the bravest thing we've ever done."

"I know," he said, his voice thin. "It feels like it. Meg, what'll I say?"

They were within several feet of Jeannette now, and Meg whispered, "Just tell her what you feel, Dad."

Jeannette's eyes brimmed with tears as they focused on Paul.

He stopped and began in a rush, "Jeannette, I was going to..." Then, apparently deciding to change his approach, he began again. "Maybe we could...what if...oh, hell!"

The right words failing him, he simply opened his arms and closed the distance that separated them.

Jeannette flew into his embrace, buried her face against his shoulder and wept.

"I love you!" he said urgently, finally coherent. "I'm sorry. Please don't *cry!*"

With a deep sigh, Meg hurried past them to the doorway of the lounge. A loud group was just getting up from the bar to leave. The rest of the lounge was empty.

Her heart sank to her toes. Amos was gone. Maybe he had never had any intention of coming back to the room. Maybe he'd just decided to cut his losses and go home.

Home, she thought emptily. She didn't even know just where in San Francisco that was for him; they'd never talked about it. Suddenly her mind was crowded with all the things they'd never talked about, leaving her heart proportionately vacant. She put a hand over it, realizing for the first time how much emptiness could hurt.

Then a flicker of movement in the far corner caught her eye and she turned to see Amos sitting on the bench that ran along the back wall, his dark blue shirt almost disappearing against the blue-and-gray upholstery. He raised a cup to his lips then put it down again.

Deciding that she'd lived through rejection once and could probably do so again, Meg wove her way among the chairs and small tables to the corner where Amos sat. He appeared lost in thought and didn't see her until she stood on the other side of the table.

He looked up at her, his eyes anguished and weary, and she felt a terrible guilt claw at her chest. She remembered the way he'd waited for Jillian's subtle movement to throw himself at her so that he would take the bullet and not Meg.

"Loving," Frank had said, "is the bravest thing you'll ever do."

Amos studied her, his expression indeterminate. Fortunately, she'd expected him to be less than delighted to see her.

She sat down opposite him. "Hi," she said. She would have touched him, but she wasn't sure it was safe. "I just ran into Jeannette in the lobby."

He nodded, his expression polite but not precisely friendly. "We talked for a while. She and your dad were having some kind of problem."

"Yeah. I think that's over, though." She found it odd and even painful to sit across from him with this cool distance between them. They'd grown so close

in such a short time that being relegated to a point
outside his life made everything else in *her* life seem
wrong.

AMOS FOUND IT TERRIFYING to realize how important
Meg had become to him. His world had plunged into
darkness earlier when she'd said the word *annulment,*
but the moment she sat across from him, it was high
noon on a sunlit lake.

Or maybe it was just that fiery blaze before sunset.
Maybe she was here to say goodbye.

"Good," he said. "I think they'll be happy together."

"Yeah." Her voice sounded strained. "Me, too."

He wished she would get to the point of her visit,
but if she was trying to make up with him, he didn't
want to do anything to scare her off. And if she was
here to say goodbye, he didn't want to do anything
to hurry her.

So he waited.

He was watching her hands, which were knotted
together on the edge of the table, and stared as one
of them moved cautiously to cover his right hand.

When he looked up into her eyes, he found them
pleading with him.

If you're about to ask me to let you go, he thought,
the answer's no!

But she cleared her throat and said, "I've been
thinking."

Oh-oh. "Yeah?"

"Rose and Samantha," she said, and smiled trem-
ulously. "Paul and Anthony. What do you think?"

Perhaps it was his fear at the thought of losing her
that accounted for his slow reactions. "Rose and

Sam...?'' Then he noticed the light in her eyes that always appeared when she talked about the four children they would send to Harvard.

It wasn't sunset at all, but high noon!

He pushed the small table aside and stood to take her into his arms. She clung with all the fervor he could have hoped for.

"Oh, Amos, I was just scared," she said, weeping against his throat. "And I hated it, because even when I was sure no man would ever love me, I knew I still had courage. When I felt like that was gone, I..."

"But it wasn't gone," he interjected, trying to reason with her. Out of the corner of his eye he saw the bartender smile as he dried glasses. "You had every ri—"

She put a hand over his mouth.

"I know I was stupid. Just tell me you understand that I was going to leave because I *did* love you, and not because I didn't."

And this was the kind of reasoning he'd be dealing with for a lifetime. Courage, indeed.

He kissed the palm of her hand, then drew it down and held it firmly. "The only thing I want to know is that you're not leaving, and that you'll never even talk about leaving again."

She wrapped her arms around his waist with impressive strength. "I won't, I promise."

He kissed her ear. "Good. And what would you think about changing employers, considering Rose, Samantha, Paul and Anthony? You could come and set up security for me. I'd feel a lot better if you weren't putting yourself in danger on a regular basis."

Meg accepted the good sense of that suggestion

with the realization that she had added yet another protective male to her life.

She smiled up at him. "Okay. Do I get all the toys I want as the boss's wife?"

He kissed her soundly as he led her out of the lounge. "And you can play with me anytime you want."

continues with

IT TAKES A COWBOY

by

Gina Wilkins

Blair Townsend didn't know the meaning of
chaos until her holy terror of a nephew came to live
with her. Jeffrey needed a positive role model—and
Blair wasn't above buying one. Sexy-as-sin rancher
Scott McKay looked like he'd have no trouble
teaching Jeffrey how to be a man. Only Scott
seemed far more interested in showing Blair how to
be a woman....

Available in November

Here's a preview!

"I BEG YOUR PARDON?"

Scott laughed. "Have I ever mentioned that I like it when you do that?"

"When I do what?" Blair asked.

"When you act all snooty and indignant. It's cute as all-get-out. Makes me want to just kiss you silly."

While Blair fumbled for a response, Jeffrey gave a muffled laugh.

Scott grinned, apparently satisfied with her reaction. "I'll clean the fish. You can make some side dishes, if you want."

Still flustered, Blair nodded. "Of course. Jeffrey, go wash up now and change into clean clothes."

"Okay, Aunt Blair." He headed obligingly toward the door.

"If only he was always that agreeable," she murmured, mostly to herself, as she watched her nephew disappear inside. And then she turned to Scott with a frown. "I really wish you wouldn't do that."

He gave her an innocent look. "Do what?"

"Flirt with me in front of Jeffrey. You'll confuse him. He's too young to understand what you're like."

Scott drew himself up a bit straighter and rested his

hands on his hips, studying her with a deceptively bland smile. "And what *am* I like?"

She frowned at him. "You know what I mean."

"No, I'm not sure I do. Surely you aren't accusing me of being a compulsive playboy? A woman-chaser?"

"Well, I..."

"Because if I were that kind of man, I'd have done much more than call you cute and talk about wanting to kiss you. Being alone like this with a beautiful woman would be more temptation than I could resist."

Blair felt her cheeks heat. *Beautiful? Did he really think so, or was he...?* She frowned again and shook her head, telling herself he was simply being difficult. Again. "I didn't say you..."

He took a step nearer, so close he had only to lift his hand to touch her warm cheek. He seemed suddenly much bigger, his shoulders broader. He smelled of fresh air and healthy male, and the combination was incredibly enticing.

Funny. Until this moment, she'd never suspected she had a weakness for charming cowboys.

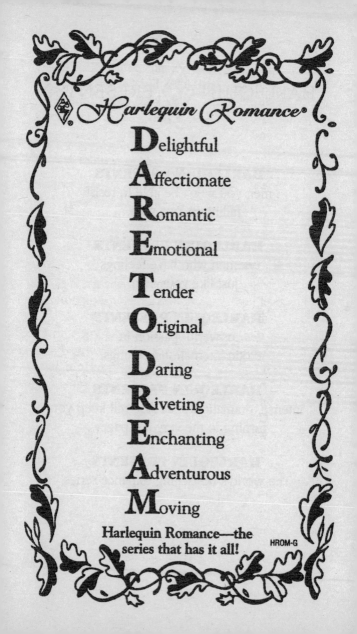

Harlequin Romance®

Delightful

Affectionate

Romantic

Emotional

Tender

Original

Daring

Riveting

Enchanting

Adventurous

Moving

Harlequin Romance—the
series that has it all!

HROM-G

HARLEQUIN PRESENTS®

HARLEQUIN PRESENTS
men you won't be able to resist
falling in love with...

HARLEQUIN PRESENTS
women who have feelings
just like your own...

HARLEQUIN PRESENTS
powerful passion in
exotic international settings...

HARLEQUIN PRESENTS
intense, dramatic stories that will keep you
turning to the very last page...

HARLEQUIN PRESENTS
The world's bestselling romance series!

**Harlequin®
Historical**

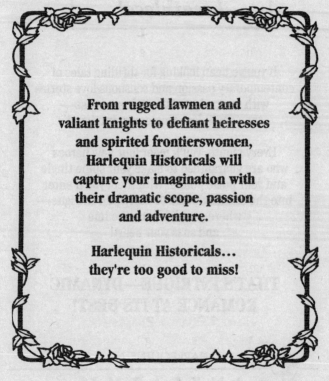

From rugged lawmen and
valiant knights to defiant heiresses
and spirited frontierswomen,
Harlequin Historicals will
capture your imagination with
their dramatic scope, passion
and adventure.

Harlequin Historicals...
they're too good to miss!

LOOK FOR OUR FOUR FABULOUS MEN!

Each month some of today's bestselling authors bring
four new fabulous men to Harlequin American Romance.
Whether they're rebel ranchers, millionaire power brokers
or sexy single dads, they're all gallant princes—and
they're all ready to sweep you into lighthearted fantasies
and contemporary fairy tales where anything is possible
and where all your dreams come true!

You don't even have to make a wish...
Harlequin American Romance will grant your every desire!

Look for Harlequin American Romance
wherever Harlequin books are sold!

HARLEQUIN SUPERROMANCE®

...there's more to the story!

Superromance. A *big* satisfying read about unforgettable characters. Each month we offer
four very different stories that range from family
drama to adventure and mystery, from highly emotional stories to romantic comedies—and
much more! Stories about people you'll
believe in and care about. Stories too
compelling to put down....

Our authors are among today's *best* romance writ-
ers. You'll find familiar names and
talented newcomers. Many of them are
award winners—and you'll see why!

If you want the biggest and best
in romance fiction, you'll get it
from Superromance!

Available wherever Harlequin books are sold.